STRANGER AT THE DOOR

STRANGER AT THE DOOR

by

Victor J. Banis

The Borgo Press
An Imprint of Wildside Press

MMVII

CONTENTS

CHAPTER ONE

Loneliness had come as a guest in the house. She hovered near the faded velvet of the draperies, peering through dust-streaked glass. She paused among Victorian ornaments and misplaced Chippendale, her fingers trailing over yellowed keys on the ancient Steinway.

She had come, Roger Caldwell thought sadly, as a guest. She would remain as mistress. He stood from the desk, his attention stubbornly refusing to remain focused on the monthly accounts, and crossed to the window, peering out without seeing anything beyond.

"I should be packing," he reminded himself, but he did not want to resume his task. The truth was, he did not want to go, to leave this house. He preferred to stand here at the draperies, nor did he mind the presence of Loneliness beside him, for he found even her company familiar and comfortable.

"Time," he said aloud, pulling himself resolutely away from the window, "Is passing." It had been passing all along, of course, swiftly, irrevocably.

Like the house, he was growing old. He felt the weight of his sixty plus years perhaps more heavily than did the house her full century. He could not even wish to be young again, for he scarcely believed that he had ever been young. That, he had finally come to realize, was the misfortune of good fortune, of being reared to wealth and position and the attendant responsibilities that had been drilled into him from childhood.

He had not been merely young Roger, but young Roger Caldwell, and he had never been allowed to overlook that difference, any more than the house had been allowed to fancy, even for a moment, that she was merely a pleasant little cottage.

He sat again at his desk, running a hand through his gray, thinning hair and frowned as he once more directed his attention to his work. He studied the bill from the market, the grocery account.

He was certain that Mr. Schaffer was overcharging him. Hadn't he quoted the steaks at a dollar twenty-nine a pound, and there they were on the bill, at a dollar forty. Another penalty for being a Caldwell.

"They can afford it," he could hear Mr. Schaffer justifying the deception to his wife.

With a resigned sigh, Roger signed his name to the check he had written and tucked it into the return envelope along with the bill. In the long run, the amount couldn't involve more than a dollar or two, and the Caldwells undoubtedly could still afford that, although Mr. Schaffer might have been shocked to discover the increasing limitations on what the Caldwells could afford.

There had been a time when there had been no limitations, a time when they had reigned in this house as Cincinnati's first family—and to Mama, they were still that, but Roger did not need his monthly struggle with the accounts to tell him that their reign was over, ten years over, that they had been replaced by families of newer and more genuine wealth—young, dynamic, often tasteless people, but people with large fortunes nonetheless.

The monthly bills taken care of, Roger carried the envelopes to the console in the hall, near the front door, where he would be sure to take them with him when he went out. He half rang for Mrs. Bruce before he remembered that the housekeeper was no longer there, that he had dismissed her days before.

Just as well, he assured himself as he moved along the dim hall toward the kitchen, going to prepare his own tea. Mrs. Bruce had been rather a bossy sort, and he himself too willing to give in, with the result that he had been very nearly a servant to her whims and moods rather than the reverse. If he had been smart, he would have let her go weeks ago, but dismissing people was a chore he had always managed to put off as long as possible. It was bad enough when you had a legitimate reason, such as closing up the house. Even so, Mrs. Bruce had managed to imply that the house was only an excuse to conceal more unreasonable motives.

He set the teakettle atop the antiquated stove, stooping to blow on the gas jet before it would come to life, and wondered if after all it wouldn't have been wiser to keep the housekeeper on until the house actually was closed. It meant only another month, and there was still so much to be done. Probably he would never get to some of it. There were the back stairs, now locked off from the rest of the house because they were flagrantly unsafe, a withered limb no longer able to play its role, and they really ought to be repaired, but they led nowhere, only to the top attic, which was empty now, so there was no reason for anyone to use them. In any case, unless you knew to look for it, the door—concealed at the back of a broom closet—was not likely even to be discovered, so no one would be tempted, though he couldn't think who that someone might be.

The furniture would all have to be covered, of course, and a few things put into storage. The morning paper carried the advertisement for the car, the last item he intended to sell before departing. After that would come his trip to Europe and his first reunion with his sister, Emily, since she had taken up residence in Paris some ten years earlier, and when he returned, it would be to another home, to the small apartment that was already prepared for him.

When his tea was brewed, Roger carried it with him into the parlor and settled himself with a book of poetry, but the poetry was no more successful at holding his attention than his other diversions had been. He was restless, strangely so, and the house was too quiet, with first Mama and now the housekeeper gone.

He made a mental note to call and see how Mama was getting along. For some peculiar reason, which he could not quite understand himself, it gave him a vague sense of annoyance to know that she was as comfortable as she seemed to be with Aunt Sarah.

Of course, Aunt Sarah and Mama were both widowed now, and Aunt Sarah's neat, modern apartment was obviously easier for both of them—

no steps to climb, a modern heating system free of the drafts that plagued this old house, everything that would make life simpler for two ladies of advancing years and bad hearts.

The front door knocker banged loudly, interrupting his train of thought. Roger sat for a moment before he remembered again that there was no Mrs. Bruce to answer it, and jumped up to get it himself.

* * * * * * *

The young man at the door was a stranger, and rather a handsome one in a crude, unpolished way. His dark hair, only half combed, framed a faced that in repose was strikingly cherubic. When he smiled, however, an oddly one-sided smile, the eyebrows arched and the dark eyes narrowed, giving him a look not at all angelic, but rather Mephistophelean.

Roger stared at him curiously, momentarily puzzled that such a perversely attractive young man should be calling on him. There had been young men, of course, sweaty cock-teasers in the darkness, in the past, but not here, never at the house. He had often wondered if someday one of those heavy-hung hustlers might not come to this very door. Faint images of the past darted through his mind—but, no, this was certainly a stranger, no one he had seen before. Not until his caller spoke did he recall the advertisement in the morning paper.

"You're the one with the car for sale?" he asked. His voice was low and the sort that seemed always to be saying something more than the actual words spoken.

The images of hustlers vanished, and Roger smiled with slight embarrassment. "Oh, yes, the car," he said. "Would you like to buy it?"

The visitor gave him another of his peculiar smiles. "I'd like to see it," he said.

"Well, that's understandable." An attractive creature, Roger thought, exciting, even. Again, memories played across Roger's consciousness. Beneath a battered corduroy jacket, the young man's shirt and trousers were unnecessarily tight fitting, but they served to reveal a well-developed physique—and a well-proportioned bulge at his crotch. "It's in the garage, back this way."

He pulled the door closed after himself and led the way around the house. The visitor walked beside him, glancing around at the grounds as they went. Roger found himself wishing that things were in better repair. The grounds were looking shabby, and they were so lovely when they were kept up.

"Nice place you have here," the young man said, seemingly unperturbed by the evidence of neglect.

"Yes. I'm fond of it, but I'm afraid it's rather too much for one person to keep up."

"You live here by yourself?" The visitor threw him a glance.

"Only for another month or so," Roger confessed, opening the gate into the back yard. "I plan to go abroad for a while, and then I suppose I'll have to think about selling the place. It's been in the family for years, but there's no one left now to keep it up. My sister lives in Paris and my mother's just too old to get around in a house like this."

"Sure seems a shame." The young man stopped by the pool, long empty, and stared down at the layer of debris and dirt at the bottom. "Must have been quite a place in its day."

They went to the garage. Roger opened the door, trying to conceal the effort necessary to lift the considerable weight, and flicked on the naked bulb that hung inside.

"It's the Packard I'm selling, the town car. I'll keep the Ford to use when I get back, although to tell you the truth, I don't really use either of them much."

The stranger walked slowly about the Packard, looking it over. It was an older model, dating back to a period of tall rooflines and sweeping fenders. At the moment it was plainly in need of cleaning and waxing, but otherwise it was sound.

"How does it run?"

"Oh, quite smoothly. The key is in the ignition, if you'd like to start it up."

He waited as the young man slid inside the car and started up the engine. He let it run for a moment or two, listening with a cocked ear.

"Not bad," he said, switching off the engine and climbing out again. Once more he circled the car to examine the exterior.

Roger stood in awkward silence. He hated the bother of selling things and hoped that the young man wouldn't want to haggle. Perhaps if he did not want to buy the car, Roger would simply call a dealer and let him take it away.

The young man finished his inspection, but he still had not offered any decision. Roger cleared his throat nervously.

"Perhaps you'd like to come inside," he suggested timidly. "We could discuss the matter over a glass of sherry." It was probably not an orthodox way to settle these things, he was thinking, but somehow it seemed to him a far more refined way of doing business.

No, there was something more than that, he admitted. Suddenly he was lonely, and did not want to re-enter the silent, empty house alone. He did not really care if his visitor bought the car or not. He could always dispose of that somehow, but something about the young man had stirred long dormant feelings within him. He had been called back to the past, to the other young men with whom he had shared a few brief moments of fleshly pleasures. Of course, this interlude would not be the same as those others had been, but at least he could talk for a while, over some sherry, and perhaps he could enjoy vicariously a few moments of youth.

"Sounds like a good idea to me," the young man said. "By the way, I'm Lenny." He offered a hand and a grip that was almost painfully strong.

"Roger Caldwell. We can go through the back way."

He led the way into the house, annoyed with himself for the tingle of excitement he had felt at Lenny's handshake. After all, this young man was here on business, he reminded himself—and anyway, Roger could not allow, had never allowed himself to contemplate such indiscretions here in Cincinnati, where he was known and where the family name was still of some, albeit diminishing, importance.

They moved through the house slowly, pausing often as Lenny admired a room or a particular piece of furniture. Roger smiled and was pleased that the house should receive the flattering attention of this pleasant young man.

In the parlor, Roger reached for a decanter of sherry, and paused. This man was of a different sphere, he reminded himself, and probably different tastes. "Perhaps you'd prefer something else?" he suggested.

"Do you have any beer?"

Roger shook his head regretfully. "Scotch?"

"Fine."

That settled, they seated themselves in the tall chairs that flanked the window, facing one another. Lenny had removed his jacket and Roger found it increasingly difficult not to let his eyes fix themselves on his bulging crotch, or wander up and down the length of the sculptured young body.

"You're a native of Cincinnati?" Roger asked.

Lenny shook his head almost apologetically. "No, I come from the West Coast. I was on my way to New York, but somebody told me Cincinnati was the Queen City, so I decided to check it out." He laughed, revealing slightly uneven teeth. Roger laughed with him, a bit uncertain as to the reason for his mirth.

Lenny grew quickly serious again, his moods passing like light and shadow over his face. "To tell the truth, I was broke," he said. "My money ran out, so I stopped here to pick up some work. That was seven months ago, and I'm still here."

"What sort of work do you do?"

"You name it. I was working on a construction job out of town a ways, but that ended last week. Right now I'm looking around for something else to do."

It struck Roger as odd that a young man without a job and admittedly short on money would be shopping for a car, but that was hardly his concern, so long as he was paid for the car.

As though reading his thoughts, Lenny said, "I have a friend, a woman. I think she may loan me the money to buy a car."

Roger said nothing, but he did not have to question how Lenny intended to repay such a load. He had known such men, gigolos who screwed anything for cash. They were more common in New York, where he had often visited in the past, but they were not unknown here in Cincinnati either.

"That's about the situation," Lenny said aloud, with a rueful grin.

Roger jumped, startled. "What's that?"

"What you were thinking, about my woman friend."

Roger wondered if the young man were indeed reading his mind. It was certainly unnerving, to have his thoughts put into words.

Lenny shifted his position in the chair. "I was broke when I arrived in town, totally broke. I met— this woman. She has money, so I let her spend some of it on me." He spoke defensively, almost defying Roger to offer some objection.

"I hadn't intended to pry," Roger apologized, not quite sure why he should find it necessary to do so. "I'm sure you're not normally the sort who enjoys being, well, dependent upon other people."

16

Lenny relaxed slightly at that. "Sorry," he said. "I guess I was trying to pick a fight over it. Some people think it's wrong of me."

Roger's discomfort was increasing. He disliked conversations of this intimacy, particularly with a virtual stranger. Yet there was something about his companion that was too direct for conventional barriers, something that created its own aura of intimacy.

"You must be lonely," Lenny said unexpectedly. It was a direct statement, rather than a question, delivered with a bold stare.

"Lonely?"

"Living here all by yourself, in this big house."

"Yes, I suppose I am." Some sixth sense warned Roger that he should employ discretion, yet the conversation seemed to be drifting quite beyond his control. The sherry, and the bluntness of his guest, had weakened his usual caution. "I used to travel. Once a month or so, I'd go into New York City."

"Used to?"

Roger hesitated, but his reserve was no longer sufficient to hold back his words. "I had some difficulty on one visit, a few years ago. I stopped going."

"A guy?"

Roger jumped again, genuinely embarrassed. Had his admiration for the young man's good looks been so obvious? "Why do you ask that?" he stammered, knowing that his embarrassment could only serve as a confirmation of Lenny's guess.

Lenny grinned, seemingly unperturbed by this turn of the conversation. "They say it takes one to know one," he said.

"I see." Roger was at a loss exactly what he should say. Deny it, he thought impulsively, though that seemed a futile gesture. And, if his guest were truly of the same caste....

"What sort of trouble?" By now the conversation was Lenny's, steered deftly into whatever channel he chose.

"A young man, I met him at a cocktail party...." As he spoke, Roger found himself reliving the experience. He seemed to be speaking more to himself than to his companion, his voice going on almost in a monotone....

* * * * * *

It was, unquestionably, a successful party. The guests had overflowed into the hall, the chatter and babble of cocktail conversation audible even in the elevator as it ascended from the lobby. Roger paused outside the apartment for a moment, never quite comfortable facing such large crowds, although it was hardly a new experience for him. He became aware of a pair of young men standing nearby in the hall and looking him over. He glanced briefly in their direction: effeminate, flamboyant types with made-up eyes and cheap, flashy clothes.

"Hello, dear," one of them greeted him with a broad smile, mistaking Roger's glance for flirtation.

Roger did not need to be told that it was something other than his looks, which had never been spectacular, which interested them. At least he could give them credit for recognizing good taste when they saw it, and expensive clothes. Of course, these young men were like many others in that respect:

such knowledge was their stock in trade. As far as that went, he was rather accustomed to being sized up in terms of his probable financial worth rather than his worth as an individual.

He knew that his success on his visits to New York depended to a large extent upon the fact that he exuded wealth and breeding. The clearly expensive suits he wore, the diamond on his finger, the brilliance of the emerald links, the car and driver he rented for his visits, the tower suite at the Waldorf—these were the elements that made up his appeal.

He minded, of course, as one always minds, but he had long since abandoned any illusions to the contrary. In his quiet way, he used these accoutrements to gain his objectives. It was the way the game was played, and he had learned to use the young men who were drawn to him as selfishly as they attempted to use him.

So he had not taken offense at the interest these two young men had taken in him. He had, however, learned through experience that he could do better, and just as he sought the best in his clothing, his jewelry, his drinks, he had made it a point to purchase with his wealth the best young men available.

Someday, of course, that would not be possible. His wealth was diminishing, he was altogether too aware of that fact. At home, in Cincinnati, he had begun to learn the niceties of economizing, but here in New York, he could still maintain the front of elegance and limitless finances. No one here need know that this trip, for the first time, he had traveled coach class.

He gave the two young men a nod, not coldly, but sufficiently distant to dash any hopes they might be entertaining, and made his way into the apartment. He steered his way deftly about elbows and trays, eventually finding himself a martini and a place by one wall where he could stand relatively safe from splashed drinks or clumsy feet.

There was simply no point in trying to find his host. He had been to Rudy's parties before. Somewhere in this crush of people, Rudy would be holding court, as was his way, fancying himself as something slightly more regal than what he truly was.

"The truth is," Roger thought ruefully, staring about at a room furnished with considerable expense and very little taste, "He's got more money than I." He could gain some satisfaction, however, from the fact that he was probably the only one aware of this. Rudy's money was "new," and considerable, and he spent it lavishly, particularly on just such entertaining as this, but those people who knew them both would invariably single out Roger as representative of the aristocratic class. He was listed in social registers and *Who's Who*, he maintained an aura of elegance that made Rudy's flashy spending seem shabby and vulgar.

Ordinarily, Roger would find a party of Rudy's amusing. In his position, Roger had learned at an early age that he must be careful and discreet. New York was an outlet for him, yet he could scarcely stand about on street corners. Thus when he had met Rudy through family acquaintances, and they had discerned their mutual inclinations, Roger had welcomed the friendship. Rudy had been invaluable in providing him ways and places for meeting people, especially the handsome young men who were always in evidence here at this apartment, and always available for someone of apparent means.

Today, however, Roger found himself largely unamused. He was out of sorts and impatient with the people who occasionally bumped or shoved against him in passing. Like cattle, he found himself thinking, boisterous people who drank too much and talked too much.

He raised his arm to glance at his watch, wondering if he should stay. As he did so, his arm bumped someone and the drink in his hand spilled.

"Oh, I'm terribly sorry," he exclaimed. The man whose jacket had received the wet offering looked pointedly at him. Roger blushed, feeling as much an oaf as the people he had been so contemptuous of a moment before. Where had the man come from anyway? He was sure there had been so one standing there earlier.

"That's all right." The stranger glanced over his shoulder, trying to survey the damage. "I shouldn't have been standing on top of you. It's just that there's so damned many people here."

"Yes, I was thinking that too. But look, I've stained your jacket. Let me see if I can do anything with it." He took his handkerchief from his pocket and dabbed at the spot, without much success.

"It's all right, really," the man insisted. He turned toward Roger, turning the wet spot from view. "You're Roger Caldwell, aren't you?"

Roger felt even more flustered now. It was silly, standing here with his handkerchief wadded in his hand, like a headwaiter or some such. For the first time, he looked the stranger in the face. It was a handsome face—no, not so much handsome as pretty, he decided on second glance. Blond hair, pale eyes, pale skin—the slightest trace of affectation would have sufficed to make him appear effeminate, but fortunately there was none.

"Yes. Have we met?" He could not place the stranger, although he was certain he would remember him if they had met before.

"Not really. I've seen you here before, at one of Rudy's parties. I'd hoped to meet you then, but I prefer an introduction, and by the time I'd managed that, you had gone. Later, I asked around about you, and found out you were from out of town. So I never really expected to meet you."

"I'm afraid this wasn't a very pleasant introduction," Roger said, indicating the drink in his hand. "But I'm flattered that you remembered me. And I'm afraid you have the advantage."

"I'm sorry. I'm Andrew Best," he said, smiling warmly and showing just the faintest of dimples.

They shook hands. "Best? Not the Vermont Bests, by any chance?"

"No, I'm afraid not," he answered with a small laugh and an almost apologetic tone.

A pleasant young man, Roger was thinking. Yes, this was why he came to Rudy's parties, why he had come today, to meet young men such as Andrew Best—handsome, polished, masculine. Whatever criticism one might direct at Rudy's vulgar show of wealth, it did attract some interesting people.

"But, I say," he said aloud, "I've spoiled your jacket. You must let me make it up to you."

"That's not necessary." He again stretched to peer over his shoulder, frowning as he did so. "But I do suppose it looks conspicuous. I ought to leave."

"There, you see, I've spoiled the party for you as well."

Andrew gave him another of those dazzling smiles. "To be frank, I was thinking of leaving anyway, so you haven't really spoiled anything for me."

There was an awkward pause, as though both of them were contemplating carrying the matter further.

"Then perhaps you'll let me give you a lift," Roger suggested finally. Ordinarily he was not so abrupt. He would wait until much had been established through conversation, and often he would even wait for a second meeting. But he liked this young man, and if Andrew was leaving now, there might not be a second meeting.

"That would be nice, thank you," Andrew said.

It was at this point that Roger invariably grew nervous. In all that happened before an actual advance took place, this might have been any ordinary social meeting, and he could handle it with the inbred finesse that came from being a Caldwell.

His training as a Caldwell, however, did not extend to dealing with the fine points of a homosexual pickup. Tawdry as it sounded, he had never been able to think of this sort of thing as anything else. Having managed an introduction and set the stage, he had moved out of his element. If he were fortunate, the person he had met would be a slightly aggressive type, who would now take the initiative. If not, then he was forced to fumble and stammer and hint until he had made his desires plain.

He was rather fortunate with Andrew who, although not really aggressive, seemed to have exactly the same plans in mind. Roger's shy suggestion that Andrew stop by his suite at the Waldorf for a drink was quickly and warmly accepted, and Roger relaxed, having carried the overtures a step further without mishap, and confident by now that it would not be difficult to carry them to the hoped for conclusion.

* * * * * * *

"Pleasant," Andrew said approvingly when he saw the suite.

"Yes, I find it comfortable." Roger ordered champagne sent up, raising an eyebrow silently to ask if that was satisfactory with his guest. A quick nod told him it was.

Conversation was easy with this relaxed stranger, who seemed to be well educated and in fact even knew some of the same people Roger knew, although he insisted he did not know them well. Roger found himself wondering how intimate his guest had been with some of them. Names were mentioned of people he knew to be from the best families, men whom he had not before suspected of being inclined toward homosexual outlets.

He was relieved when Andrew spared him the necessity of broaching the subject of sex. There was little doubt that the subject was on both their minds, but as usual, Roger had been at a loss as to how to bring it up.

"Should we get more comfortable?" Andrew asked, finishing a glass of champagne. He glanced fleetingly in the direction of the bedroom.

"Yes, I'd like that," Roger said. They stood together. There was a heat in Roger's crotch and he found himself aroused at contemplating what was to follow. He gazed longingly at the young man before him—tall, slim, sensuous. With a nervous smile, Roger turned and led the way into the bedroom, Andrew following.

Roger was somewhat modest about undressing in the light, but even with the draperies closed, the room was still far form dark. A bit uncomfortably, he removed his clothing, hanging everything neatly in the closet. Andrew, too, was neat with his things, a fact that pleased Roger. The young blond did not seem modest about his nudity. He removed his under-things without hesitation, moving unembarrassed about the room. Roger found himself staring in fascination and desire.

And Andrew was very desirable, even more so than with his clothes on. His sculptured buttocks, the slim waist, the patch of gold at the base of his stomach, fired Roger's craving. He watched the long, lovely pendulum of flesh swing lazily from side to side as the young man walked.

"Better take them off, hadn't you?" Andrew suggested with a smile, indicating the shorts that Roger still wore. "No, wait, I'll do it for you."

He slid the fabric down over Roger's hips and legs, and gently grasped the rigid, bobbing evidence of Roger's desire. Then, slowly; but firmly, he pushed Roger down upon the bed, crouching above him. Roger's vision was filled with the firm surface of a stomach, hips posed and tensed, the golden jungle of curls around a rigid column of manhood moving closer. His lips parted, to be invaded by firm, warm flesh. His hands lifted to stroke the tensed buttocks.

"Gently, gently," Andrew crooned above him. His hips moved to and fro, slowly at first, the movements gradually increasing in tempo.

The blond arched his spine, leaning backward, and his hand again clasped Roger's erection, stroking it tenderly. They moved together, Roger struggling to fill himself with the offering of his beautiful companion. He choked, never very artful in these acts, and would have paused to get his breath, but the youth above him was unrelenting now, caught up in the heat of their sexuality. His hips continued to thrust, driving himself deeper and more forcefully.

Roger's own desire concentrated itself at his loins, a mounting pressure that demanded release. It grew, becoming almost unbearable. Roger wanted to cry out, but could not. He writhed slightly, thrusting himself upward into the tight-gripping, coaxing hand.

He struggled against the weight of his partner's loins, wanting to tell him to delay. Not yet, he wanted to cry out, but the young man over him would not retreat and suddenly it was too late. Roger felt the surge of his climax, the upward rushing, and he exploded, droplets of hot liquid spattering across his abdomen.

He wanted to pause, to have a moment to regain his breath. He pushed against his partner's slim hips, but Andrew brushed his hand roughly away, and Roger realized that Andrew was near the end as well, too near to delay. His hips moved furiously now, driving deeply. Roger felt the swelling, the instant of frozen motion and then he was choking and gasping as the throbbing flesh poured out his tribute into his mouth.

Andrew fell away from him, sprawling across the bed, breathing deeply. Roger too remained motionless for a long time, his heart still pounding frantically with the exertion. Finally, Andrew moved, got up and disappeared into the bathroom. While he was gone, Roger remembered his nudity and went to the closet for a robe, slipping it on.

Andrew noticed the robe when he returned and smiled in amusement as he began to dress again. "Did you enjoy yourself?" he asked as he bent down to lace his shoes.

"Very much," Roger assured him honestly.

"That's good," Andrew said. "I always like my companions to enjoy the experience. That way, they don't object when I ask for something in the way of a reward."

A wave of disappointment swept over Roger. Of course, he had expected that this young man had a financial interest in him. That was to be expected. Ordinarily, he offered his companion some money, a few dollars to compensate for their time and the attention they had given him. He knew, after all, that he was no beauty. He did not like them to ask for it, however. Somehow, when he offered the money as a gift, it made the business seem less like prostitution.

"Of course," he answered, taking his billfold from the dress. "I had planned on offering you a little something. Will twenty do?"

Andrew straightened up. He was smiling again, but this time his smile was cold and hard, vastly different from the way he had looked at Roger before. "I had a little more than that in mind," he said bluntly.

"I see." Roger's embarrassment deepened. He had never before been in the position of haggling like this. "Fifty, then. It's steep, but I suppose I can't really object."

"I was thinking more in terms of, let's say, a thousand." Andrew stood, looking even taller than before. He was no longer pretty and gracious, but formidable and threatening.

Roger stared in astonishment. "You can't be serious," he said, "I have no intention of paying you that sort of money."

"I am serious. And you will pay. I know your type, you see. You're not the sort who likes a lot of ugly scandal, and scenes in hotels. That's the alternative you have."

Roger could scarcely believe his ears. And yet, as he met the hard gaze of the man before him, he knew that Andrew was indeed serious, in both his demands and his threats....

* * * * * * *

"You told the police about it?" Lenny asked, leaning forward in his chair. He seemed angered by the account, and full of sympathy.

"No, I couldn't, don't you see?" Roger sighed as he remembered the humiliation and the indignation he had suffered. "I couldn't afford to. He knew who I was, and it might have gotten back to someone here, and caused such a bother. The family's well known, for one thing. And my mother's had a bad heart for several years. If there had been only myself to consider, I might have dealt with it differently, but there's no telling what a scandal of that sort would do to her in her condition. I had no choice but to pay him the money he demanded, but after that I no longer had any desire to stay in New York, or pay another visit. Once burned, as they say."

"So now you just stay around here, all by yourself, in this big old house?"

"Yes. Oh, I have my occupations, of course, but not that sort of thing, not since then."

"That's too bad." Lenny seemed quite suddenly to have lost interest in the subject. He finished his drink and stood up. "I guess I'd better be going."

Roger stood also, disconcerted by the abruptness of the change. "Have you thought about the car?" he asked. It occurred to him that they had, after all, not even touched upon the subject of Lenny's visit.

"I'd like to think about it. Could I come by again tomorrow after I've talked to my friend?"

"But of course. I've enjoyed our little visit."

Lenny was smiling as he again clasped Roger's hand, this time less forcefully. "So have I," he said.

Roger stood at the door as his guest made his way down the drive. Now that the conversation was ended, he was suffering regrets at having said so much. He had in fact revealed his most embarrassing secret to this stranger, while he in turn knew little about the young man who was just leaving. He was suddenly frightened and anxious.

Lenny reached the end of the drive and paused, turning back to smile and wave. Roger returned the gesture and his fear vanished as quickly as it had come.

He was foolish to worry, he chided himself. There was scant likelihood that Lenny would be mingling with any of the Caldwell's friends, and in any event, he was such a nice young man, so open and direct, and yet thoughtful, and…he would not let himself think the other adjective that had attempted to creep into his mind…so attractive.

CHAPTER TWO

The memory of the handsome young stranger and his bulging crotch stayed with Roger throughout the evening. He had known many men like Lenny, young creatures who lived, as long as possible, on their looks and their ability to charm. Yet Lenny somehow seemed different from the others, in some way Roger could not quite define. Something about him had seemed more direct, more clear cut, and he had been, for all the weaknesses of character he might possess, a thoroughly likeable boy.

"Or is it only because I'm so alone?" Roger wondered aloud. Was he only clinging to a few moments of companionship, that had brightened his day considerably? He would have liked to invite his guest to spend the evening, even if nothing had come of it. Sex was no longer so important to him. Not that he didn't still feel the urge, and he was still physically capable, but more than anything else, he longed for a companion, someone of a nature similar to his own. It had been a long time, since that that last trip to New York City, since he had been able to fully relax with anyone, and be himself.

He found himself wondering if Lenny really would come again the following day. He hoped so.

* * * * * * *

He still hoped so when he got up in the morning, and even while he chided himself that he was being silly, he spent a great part of the morning puttering about the house, attempting to make it look slightly more presentable. He called the market and recited a list of things he would like delivered. Most of them, in fact, were things he did not really need, but included in the list was one item that had occurred to him the night before.

"Beer?" Mr. Schaffer repeated, sounding puzzled.

"Yes. Something good." Even though he knew he could not be seen, Roger felt embarrassed that the simple order should have caused comment.

"Funny," Mrs. Schaffer said, "All these years I've never known you to be a beer drinker."

"Maybe it just slipped your mind," Roger said, a bit peevishly, although it was true that he had never ordered beer before, had not even tasted it since his initial experience with it twenty or more years earlier. "Can you suggest a good brand?"

"Becks, I guess," Mr. Schaffer said. "Dark or light?"

"Send me a six pack of each," Roger said decisively.

* * * * * * *

His nervousness mounted as the afternoon wore on, and when the doorbell finally did ring, about four, he went to answer it with all the breathless excitement of a first date.

"Hi, me again," Lenny greeted him with an ingratiating smile. "I was here yesterday, remember?"

"But of course, I remember. Come in," Roger fairly gushed. He held the door wide and was flattered that Lenny went straight to the parlor, which told him Lenny had clearly remembered the previous day as well.

"Would you like a beer?" Roger asked, trying to make it sound casual and nothing out of the ordinary.

Lenny was appropriately surprised. "I thought you didn't keep it around?" he said.

"Oh, yes. I was just out yesterday, but I've stocked up since then."

He brought the beer from the kitchen, one for each of them. When he returned, Lenny was standing by the mantle, running his fingers admiringly over the porcelain clock that stood there.

"It's quite old," Roger said, causing Lenny to jump and turn about quickly as though caught in some dreadful deed. "I'm sorry, I didn't meant to startle you," Roger said.

"I just didn't hear you come back," Lenny said, relaxed again. He took the offered beer and sat in the same chair he had used the day before. "It's a beautiful clock, isn't it? Must be worth quite a bit."

Roger shrugged and sat down as well. He had far more interesting things on his mind than an old clock that had been in his family for generations. "I suppose it is. Well, here's to your health." He toasted his young guest and pretended to savor the sip he took from his beer.

Lenny's eyes went about the room. He seemed ill at ease, a sharp contrast to the relaxed manner of his previous visit, and Roger found himself fearing perhaps he had been too forward. It had seemed, though, as if they had been developing a friendship.

"You seem a bit down today," he said aloud. "Is anything wrong?"

Lenny gave him a curious look, distant and expressionless; then his face relaxed again into a smile and he shrugged. "I don't know. I guess it's just meeting you, and all."

"Meeting me?" Roger was dismayed to think that in some way he might have offended his visitor. "Have I said or done anything to make you unhappy?"

"Oh, no, nothing like that. It's just, well, when I left here yesterday, I was thinking how nice you were, and how sad it was that you are all alone here, and lonely. And the more I thought about it, the more I realized how alike we are. I mean, I've been so lonely most of my life, only I never like to admit it to myself."

"But, I thought you had a friend, that lady...."

"Oh, sure," Lenny said without enthusiasm. "We have sort of a thing going, but you know what that's like. I don't have any real friends. No one seems to like me, I mean, really like me, for myself, you know what I mean. It's always just for what they can get out of me."

"Yes, I know what you mean," Roger said thoughtfully. "I've felt the same thing myself, often. But it should be different for you. Why, you're a very likable person, you impressed me as being intelligent, you're young, and good-looking...."

"Do you think I'm good-looking?" Lenny interrupted him with a disarming frankness.

"Oh my, yes." Roger blushed like a schoolboy and stammered, "Yes, of course, I think you're quite good-looking."

Lenny beamed, obviously pleased by the reply. "Funny," he said, "I got the opposite impression. Like, yesterday, when I was here, I kept dropping hints, letting you know that I was, you know, the same way as you. And you didn't pick up on them at all. I kept sitting here thinking how great it would be to have someone like you for a friend—a special friend, you know, only, you just didn't seem interested."

Roger felt a wave of tenderness wash over him as he stared at the young man. "I'm sorry you thought that," he said softly, scarcely daring to believe the way the conversation was going. "It's just that, you see, I've been trained all my life not to make a display of my feelings. It's part of being raised the way I was. And, of course, being the way I am—the way you are, if I understand you rightly—one has to be so careful. But, contrary to the impression I seem to have given, I was quite taken by you."

They regarded one another in silence for a moment. "Do you want me?" Lenny asked.

My, that is certainly blunt, Roger thought. *Too blunt*, a warning voice sounded faintly in his mind.

Across from him, Lenny parted his legs—firmly muscled legs encased in tight, faded jeans, legs that formed a V that carried the eye upward to a bulge that already looked slightly swollen. Lenny smiled sardonically as he saw where Roger's eyes went. He was such an attractive young man, Roger found himself thinking, and so nice—surely there could be no danger here.

"Yes," Roger answered his question, his voice so faint that he scarcely heard the word himself.

Lenny stood, moving slowly across the room. His hand went to the opening of his jeans, fumbling with the button and the zipper there until they were open. Roger held his breath as the desired flesh was tugged into view—splendid, erect, exciting him as he had not been excited in years.

"We'd better go to my room" Roger said hoarsely. Lenny was standing directly in front of him now, legs apart, cock stretching out blatantly before him.

"This is okay," Lenny said, quietly but confidently. He reached for Roger, his fingers light but firm on Roger's head, pulling him forward. Roger yielded, too eager to argue the point. No one could see, unless they were actually trespassing on the lawns, staring in the windows—and no one ever came here.

He opened his mouth greedily and it was quickly filled with the warm, sweet flesh, brushing against his lips. It had been so long! His heart pounded in his chest, he wanted to rip away his own trousers, but he restrained himself. Later, he was sure, Lenny would take care of him. For now, there was only the statue-like form before him, the hard flesh in his mouth. Lenny stood with legs parted, one hand on a hip, the other holding Roger's head firmly. His hips pushed forward, his knees bent, thrusting himself eagerly toward his partner.

Roger stared with wide open eyes, feasting on every part of the body that was within his vision. He could see the very base of Lenny's cock, and in the opening of the jeans, a nest of raven colored hair. Higher, where the jeans fell open at the waist, was a patch of firm, smooth flesh. He reached out and ran a finger lightly over Lenny's abdomen.

"Suck it," Lenny whispered frantically above him. He buried himself deeply, withdrew, lunged forward once again. As his lust grew, his movements became wilder and he nearly lost his balance. He leaned forward, over Roger, bracing himself against the wings of the chair behind Roger's head, and drove in and out steadily, powerfully. Roger caught the strong, thickly muscled legs in his arms, clinging to them deliriously.

"Hang on," Lenny cried aloud. His body tensed, the muscles in his legs becoming rock hard. He shook wildly and then, swept away in the fervor of his climax, threw himself forward, flinging them both back against the chair. The spurt of his juices seemed to last forever, until Roger felt that he must breathe or die in the throes of this young animal's passion.

The weight moved from him at last, Lenny righting himself again, although less steadily. He threw his head back, gasping for air.

"Whew," he said at last, smiling happily down at the man who had provided his pleasure, "You're a hungry one, aren't you?"

Roger was still too short of breath to speak. He smiled upward, happy to have given so much pleasure. His own cock was still hard, his blood tingling with excitement. Lenny glanced down and saw his arousal.

"Look, why don't you go head and take care of that?" he suggested, tucking himself back into his jeans and tugging up the zipper again. "I won't mind."

Roger suppressed his disappointment. He had expected Lenny to repay the favor, but of course he knew that most men, once they had achieved their own climax, had no further desire for sex play. Perhaps later, when he was aroused again, Lenny would feel more inclined.

"No, that's all right," Roger said aloud, adjusting his trousers as well as possible to conceal the display. "I think I need to catch my breath."

Lenny laughed slightly, pleasantly. "Yeah, I know what you mean. Cigarette?"

"No, thanks," Roger said. "Would you like another beer?"

"Sure." Lenny seated himself in the chair again. It was almost as though nothing had occurred to interrupt the earlier scene.

Roger hummed to himself as he went to fetch the beer. It had not been complete, but it had been quite enjoyable nonetheless. A bit dangerous, to be sure. It was the first time in his life he had done any such thing here in Cincinnati, let alone in his own home, but he felt that there was little risk. In the past, there had always been others here in the house—his mother, the servants—but now there was no one around to walk unexpectedly into the room. And Lenny was hardly the sort to leave and divulge the story to the local newspapers or anything like that. Almost regretfully, he admitted to himself that he probably would never see Lenny again after today.

"I quite forgot about the car," he said as he returned to the parlor with Lenny's beer. "Did you decide you wanted it?"

Lenny seemed to have forgotten the purpose of his visit as well. "Oh, yes. I think so, anyway. I was wondering, actually, if you'd mind my mechanic taking a look at it. I don't know too much about motors and things, and I'd feel better if I knew what he thought about it."

"Why of course," Roger said, "Send him around whenever you like." He handed Lenny his beer and gave one young knee a fond pat.

Lenny sipped the beer thoughtfully, frowning slightly. "That's the problem," he said. "You see, he works this garage by himself, so it's a little hard for him to get away. I wondered if maybe I could take it over to him."

Roger considered the suggestion for a moment, but he could find nothing objectionable in the suggestion. Certainly Lenny was entitled to have his own mechanic look the car over, and he was certain that the car would be in good hands. Lenny was such a thoughtful young man, after all.

"You could come with me, of course," Lenny said, seeing Roger's hesitation. For a moment, Roger nearly accepted the invitation. "I just thought," Lenny said, "Well, you know, the two of us running around together, the difference in our ages—people do have dirty minds, don't they?"

He was right, Roger knew that at once, and was grateful to Lenny for his discretion. It was one thing for them to engage in love making here in the house, in private, where no one would ever know, but it would be foolish for him to be seen about town in the company of someone so young, and so obviously not of his class. He would certainly be seen, people here knew him, and some of them were bound to question the friendship.

"That won't be necessary," he said aloud. "Why don't you take it along and see what he has to say. I'm sure he'll give it a clean bill of health."

"Great, I appreciate that," Lenny said. He looked so genuinely pleased, and happy, that Roger was glad he had agreed to the suggestion. Besides, he was looking forward to Lenny's return, and a possible show of gratitude. It was certainly proving to be a most enjoyable business deal, this car selling.

* * * * * * *

It was a strange experience to stand at the door and watch the old Packard move slowly and gracefully down the drive. No one but Roger himself had driven it in at least ten years, and Roger even had a fleeting and silly impression that the car might not approve of being handed over to someone else.

He noted, however, that Lenny handled the car smoothly and carefully. Roger had taken pains to point out the car's idiosyncrasies—it was not like the modern ones, with power this and power that, though it did have an automatic transmission, and turn signals. It had been built, however, for the comfort of the passengers rather than the driver, and designed for elegance.

He returned to the parlor in a happy daze. It had been an exciting experience, sex with Lenny, and Lenny had even hinted that there would be more to come. Of course, Roger was not enough of a fool to imagine that anymore more could come of it than a few torrid, maddening sessions of sex. He had reconciled himself to that inevitable state of affairs many years before, but he had also learned to enjoy the pleasure to the fullest when it was available to him.

He removed the beer bottles to the kitchen, rinsed them and placed them carefully in the garbage, and wondered whether Lenny liked cocktails. It was late afternoon already, and martinis would not be remiss when Lenny returned. Of course, he reminded himself, Lenny had not really said when he would be back, but then, he was to a degree at the mercy of the schedule of his mechanic friend.

Surely it would not be more than an hour. He glanced at the large wall clock. It was almost five. Yes, by six o'clock, cocktails would definitely be in order—and dinner. Perhaps he ought to invite his new friend to stay for dinner. Mrs. Bruce…he caught himself, remembering that there was no Mrs. Bruce any longer.

"Well, I'm not completely helpless," he said aloud. He made a quick inventory of what he had on hand: lamb chops, a few frozen items, some greens for a salad. Yes, he could put together a satisfactory dinner without much effort.

Excited by the prospect of cooking for Lenny, Roger busied himself getting things ready. He set up the dining room. It was more bother, but, really, there was nothing quite so nice as a dinner served in the proper surroundings, was there? The silver needed some polishing, and it was necessary to wash and polish the crystal. He worked hard and fast to make the room as lovely as possible. When he glanced at the clock again, it was nearly six.

Good Heavens, he thought hurrying more than ever. He set out the food so that it could be prepared in a matter of minutes. From the wine closet he produced a good bottle of Bordeaux, not quite his best, but one that would surely be savored. Then he hurried to his room to fresh up a bit.

By the time he had gotten himself ready, clean and in fresh clothes, and nicely scented, it was almost six thirty. "It's a good thing he's a bit late," he thought, returning to the kitchen where he mixed a pitcher of martinis. This way, he managed to get the stage all set before his guest arrived. It occurred to him briefly that Lenny might not be able to stay for dinner. He did have "a friend," after all. Still, Lenny had hinted that he would stay for a little while when he returned, and Roger was confident that, when he saw everything in readiness for a lovely dinner, Lenny would be persuaded.

He took a cocktail with him and made his way to the parlor. It was nearly dark now. He would be glad when summer was truly here, and the light lasted longer. He switched on a lamp and tried to read, but his attention kept wandering from the book and back to memories of Lenny's firm cock.

The hall clock struck seven, sounding louder than was usual. Roger frowned and stared at the window, beyond which it was not truly dark. Had he shown Lenny how to operate the headlights? He couldn't remember. Perhaps there had been an accident. Perhaps he ought to call….but he remembered that he had not even thought to ask Lenny's phone number, or his address.

"Stupid of me," he said aloud, his book forgotten on his lap. "Suppose he meant to steal the car…?" He quickly pushed that thought aside. Lenny was hardly the sort and anyway, that wasn't the way people went about stealing cars. They broke into them on the streets, or something like that. They didn't come to one's home and just ask if they could take it away. Why, this way, he could tell the police….he hesitated. Tell them what? He knew only the name Lenny. He could certainly provide a description—tall, about six foot, magnificent build, good legs, very handsome in a mischievous way, a sensuous mouth….

"I'm being perfectly silly," he scolded himself, annoyed with this train of thought. He took up his book resolutely and began to read again, forcing himself to concentrate on the letters before him, although they made little if any sense.

By eight o'clock he was genuinely worried. Surely it couldn't take three hours to drive the car to a mechanic and have it checked over? Now that he thought of it, Lenny had not mentioned what garage, or where it was—but Cincinnati wasn't that large a city. In an hour or so, one should be able to drive across it and back.

He had long since finished his martini, and had a second one. He began to pace the floor nervously. Should he call the police? There would be all that bother, and probably it would even hit the papers, and he would look so stupid. They would want to know what he knew about this young man with the sensuous mouth, and why he had so trustingly handed over a valuable car to a stranger. Perhaps the other part of it would even come out, and there would be a scandal. He shuddered at the prospect.

Suppose there had been an accident? Suppose Lenny were hurt, and couldn't get in touch with him? Was there anything in the car that would identify the car's owner? He thought for a moment: the registration certificate, of course, but would they check that, or would they assume that the car belonged to the driver?

The hall clock struck nine. I really should do something, Roger thought anxiously, but what? Call mother? No, that wouldn't do. She would only get upset, and the doctors had warned him at great length about her heart. The slightest upset could be disastrous. Anyway, there was nothing she could do about the car.

It was well on the way to nine thirty when the phone rang, startling Roger with its unexpected shrillness. It rang so seldom. He hurried to answer it, scarcely daring to think about who it might be.

"Mr. Caldwell?" the voice on the line asked.

"Yes?" Was that his voice? So hard to tell on the phone. It was similar—or was it?

"This is Mr. Brook, from the travel agency. I hope you don't mind my calling at this hour, but I wanted to clear up a few details with you while I'm working on your trip."

"Oh, I see. No, it's all right, I was still up." Roger was only dimly aware of the voice droning on and on, something about his reservations for the trip to Europe. Why couldn't the stupid man have written to him about it? He loathed doing business on the phone anyway, and at the moment he had other things on his mind than the question of which hotel he preferred in Paris.

"Yes, that will be fine," he said impatiently into the mouthpiece, in answer to some question he had only half heard. "Whatever you think best will be satisfactory, I'm sure. I came to you with the matter so that I wouldn't be bothered with a lot of details."

"We only want to be sure you're happy with the arrangements, sir," the voice on the phone whined, apparently offended by the tone Roger had used.

"I'm quite happy with them, I'm sure," Roger insisted. "Yes, quite happy."

He had scarcely returned the receiver to the cradle when the phone rang again. He snatched it up, almost suspecting that it was the gentleman from the travel agency again, and prepared to be quite annoyed.

This time, however, it was Lenny. Now that he heard it again, he recognized the voice immediately.

"Roger? This is Lenny. Remember, I came about the car?"

"Yes, yes, of course. Where are you? I've been concerned about it...."

He noticed, for the first time, the sounds in the background. One thing was certain: wherever Lenny was, he was decidedly not at a garage. There was the sound of music, loud and raucous, and a babble of voice, laughing and shouting. It sounded like a rather boisterous party.

"I got tied up," Lenny said calmly, seemingly not at all perturbed by Roger's concern. "My mechanic was busy when I took it to him, so I waited and then brought it by his house."

"I see. You'll be bringing it along now, then?" From the background noises, Roger could not help but wonder if the mechanic was in any condition to look over a car.

"Well...." Lenny hesitated. "What I thought was, why don't I wait until morning? He still hasn't looked at it, you see. I thought I'd let him see it in the morning, and then I'd bring the car back."

"Oh." Roger was taken aback by the suggestion. It was presumptuous, to say the least, and he was annoyed anyway that the evening had turned out so badly. "I don't know," he said peevishly.

"Well, if you want, I could bring it back now and drop it off real quick. Of course, I was thinking, that if I brought it back tomorrow morning, I could stay and spend some time with you, maybe even the whole day. I sure enjoyed our little visit today."

The last was delivered in a different tone of voice, more intimate, although Roger was certainly aware to what he referred.

"Of course, if you need the car tonight...."

"No, I don't need it, actually...."

Roger thought for a moment. Charming or not, Lenny was certainly a brazen young man. Well, he could insist that the car be delivered immediately, but that would not accomplish anything but some bad feelings—and if he agreed to Lenny's suggestion, then Lenny would undoubtedly be grateful tomorrow. And maybe, Roger thought, I am just being peevish.

"I suppose tomorrow will be all right," he said with a sigh. "Incidentally, do you have a phone where I can reach you? I neglected to get that earlier." That would show that he wasn't taking this business lightly.

"Sure," Lenny said without hesitation, and gave him the number. Roger wrote it down.

"I'll see you in the morning, then," Roger said.

"Great. Wait'll you see how much I appreciate it. I almost wish I could spare more time tonight. I keep thinking about this afternoon."

There was another voice just then, muffled but loud, the voice of a woman obviously quite near the phone. The sounds got more muffled, as though Lenny had put his hand over the phone, but the sound of a woman's loud laughter was still unmistakable. Then, Lenny was back on the line again. "I'll see you tomorrow, then," he said, and the connection was broken abruptly, without even a good-bye.

Roger stared at the instrument for a long moment in silence. Perhaps he had been foolish. He knew nothing about this young man, after all, except that he was attractive, and he had seemed so nice.

I should eat something, he thought glumly, returning the phone to its cradle. He wasn't thinking very clearly—the martinis, the lack of food, and all that worrying. Lenny was young, after all, and apparently just a little thoughtless. That wasn't an unusual trait in the young, and he had offered to bring the car back right now, so he obviously wasn't trying to steal it. For that matter, if he were attempting anything untoward, he wouldn't have called at all, nor would he have given out a phone number at which he could be reached.

Roger looked at the number he had written on the note pad by the phone. Of course, that could be anyone's number, or even one Lenny had just made up on the spur of the moment. He half reached for the phone to try the number, and checked himself. That would prove nothing. Obviously Lenny wasn't at home. He was at some sort of party.

The house seemed even emptier than before. Its presence hovered about him unpleasantly. He made his way to the dining room, still set up for the dinner that had not taken place. The candles flickered, casting glittering reflections on the crystal and china. The gleam of silver seemed to mock the excitement with which he had prepared the table earlier.

Grimly, Roger blew out the candles, ignoring the wax that dripped onto the cloth. It didn't matter. In a short time, the cloth would be packed away. Probably he would never use it again.

He decided that he wasn't hungry. He finished his drink, his third one, and checked to make sure the doors were locked, and made his way up the wide stairs to the second floor. Tomorrow, everything would be all right. The car would be back, and he would no longer have to worry about it.

And Lenny would be here, and for a short time, he would not be lonesome.

CHAPTER THREE

Roger woke with a dull headache. For a few minutes he yielded to the temptation to remain where he was in the cozy warmth, oblivious to the spring morning beyond the window and the sunlight that filtered through the curtains.

He remembered then that Lenny was coming this morning, with the car. At that, he shed the remnants of sleep and sat up quickly. It was nine o'clock already, and Lenny would probably be here soon. It would not do for him to appear at the door unshaven and half dressed.

Ordinarily, he would have had his coffee first thing, before preparing himself for the day. In the past, he would have rung for Mrs. Bruce and she would have appeared shortly with his coffee and a roll. Since he had dismissed her, he was unfortunately forced to descend to the kitchen in the mornings and prepare his own breakfast.

This morning, however, he shaved and showered first, leaving the bathroom door open so that he could hear the doorbell or the phone over the sound of the water. Not until he was fully dressed, selecting his clothes with special care, did he make his way down to the kitchen to brew coffee.

As it was, his haste proved to be unnecessary. By noon there was still no sign of Lenny, and Roger's anxiety of the previous evening had returned, along with considerable annoyance. He was being made a fool of, never a pleasant realization. One delay might be thoughtlessness, but a second one became a different matter.

He went to the phone, to Lenny's number written on the note pad. He hesitated for another minute, still reluctant to face problems and unpleasantness. Deciding finally that it would have to be done, he dialed the number.

He waited impatiently as the phone rang and rang, and was about to give up the attempt when the receiver on the other end was finally lifted. There was a long moment of silence before an obviously sleepy voice greeted him none too cheerfully.

"This is Roger Caldwell." Roger attempted to make his voice as firm and stern as possible, and succeeded instead in sounding somewhat petulant.

"Oh, hello," Lenny greeted him. If he felt guilty or sorry, there was no trace of it in his voice. If anything, he sounded surprised that Roger should be calling him. "What's up?"

It was Roger's turn to be surprised. He should have thought the reason for his call was obvious, even to someone who had been sleeping until noon. "It's about the car," he said. "I thought you were bringing it back this morning."

"Oh, sure. What time is it?"

"It's after twelve," Roger said a bit impatiently. This was becoming ridiculous.

"Oh, is it? I've been sleeping."

"So I gathered."

There was a faint clatter and a puff of breath that told him Lenny had lit a cigarette. "Well, look, tell you what, I'll get myself organized and then I'll take the car by the garage, and after that I'll be over."

"You mean your mechanic still hasn't seen the car?" Roger asked.

Lenny laughed and explained patiently, as if to a small child, "I've been asleep. I just now woke up."

Of course, that was logical, but it was also quite annoying. Roger could not imagine the necessity of anyone's sleeping this late, and particularly not when they had an appointment. "Then perhaps you had better forego the mechanic," he said sharply. "If you don't mind, I think I would like the car brought back."

"Sure, sure, look, this won't take long. I should be there, oh, say, by three o'clock?"

His opinion of Lenny was changing rapidly. Not only was the young man rude and presumptuous, but he could be rather dense as well. "I think not," Roger said firmly. "You've already had the car an excessively long time, it seems to me, and frankly, I'm becoming concerned. I must insist that you bring it back at once."

"Okay," Lenny said, sounding not at all perturbed. "I'm just getting up, like I said. I'll have to clean up and get some coffee. Let's make it two o'clock, okay?"

Roger sighed impatiently, no longer in the slightest degree concerned with whether he offended this impudent creature or not. "I don't seem to be making myself clear," he said. "I don't like to make threats, but...."

"What are you threatening me with?" Lenny interrupted him in a sharp voice.

Roger was taken aback by the question. "Why... why, with taking my car, of course."

"You gave me permission to take it."

"For an hour or so yesterday. It's well past that now." Such effrontery! Lenny seemed to be totally unaware that he had done anything wrong.

There was a moment of silence. "And what exactly do you plan to do?"

Roger could scarcely believe his ears. He was actually being dared to insist on having his own car back. "Why, I'll call the police," he stammered, his self-control slipping away from him. "If that car isn't here in an hour, I shall call the police and report it stolen."

"Couldn't that be a little embarrassing?"

Roger caught himself on the verge of a sharp reply. "What do you mean by that?" he asked instead, but he was already beginning to understand just what Lenny meant.

"Why, just that," Lenny said calmly. "Suppose the police did pick me up with the car. I'd have no choice but to explain how I happened to have the car. You know, all about what happened between us, and how I thought we were such close friends, and when you loaned me the car, I never dreamed you would regard it as stolen.

"This is preposterous," Roger said, but the fight had all gone from his voice. He knew full well Lenny was right. Such an incident would be highly embarrassing, to say the least.

When he spoke again, Lenny's voice was more pleasant. "Look, I don't know what we're fighting about anyway," he said. "I'm bringing your car back, so why get yourself all upset? Hell, I didn't mean to worry you or anything like that. You know I like you. I just didn't think you'd be in such a lather about it."

The change in tone was almost too much for Roger. "I…it's just that…I did want the car back, don't you see?"

"Sure, no problem. I'll have it there in a little while, I promise. Quit worrying, why don't you?"

"Fine. I'll see you a little later." Roger was quite relieved to have the conversation at an end. He was at a loss as to just what he could do anyway. Of course, if the car were really stolen, he would have to call the police, scandal or no scandal—but if Lenny really was bringing it back, even if he was late in doing so, why, no real harm had been done, had it?

He would wait, he decided, and see whether Lenny stuck to his promise to bring the car back. If he did, then everything was fine, actually, except that he had spent an unpleasant evening and morning of worry. If Lenny didn't show up…well, he would cross that bridge when he came to it.

The time dragged by at a painfully slow pace. Roger busied himself about the house, forcing himself to concentrate on the chores that needed to be done. Before he knew it, it would be time for him to leave for Europe, and at this rate, absolutely nothing would be done.

He pointedly ignored the striking of the clock, which told him it was one. He had neglected to ask even in what part of town Lenny's apartment was located. Even with the best of intentions, it took a certain amount of time to shower and shave, to dress and to drive somewhere.

When the clock struck two, he decided that there was a limit to the amount of time one needed for such routine tasks. Not quite sure what he intended to say, he went to the phone and dialed Lenny's number again. This time, although he waited for the phone to ring numerous times, there was no answer. He concluded, with some relief, that Lenny was on his way here after all.

An hour later, his relief had again turned to annoyance. He tried the number twice again, still with no results, and retired despondently to the parlor, trying to imagine what he could do without causing a great deal of unpleasantness.

So absorbed was he in his thoughts that he did not even hear the car come up the long drive. The doorbell brought him from his thoughts with a start, and when he found Lenny waiting outside, he was so relieved that he all but forgot his previous annoyance.

"Oh, hello, come in, come in," he fairly gushed, leading the way to the parlor. "Would you like a beer, or a drink?"

"No, thanks," Lenny replied in a cool voice. No doubt, Roger thought, he was pouting over having been scolded—and now that the crisis had passed, Roger actually felt a bit guilty at having made such a fuss. All's well that ends well, after all, he told himself.

"Well," he said aloud, twisting his hands together awkwardly, "What did your mechanic think of the car?" He was at a loss as to how to restore the pleasant camaraderie that had existed between them on Lenny's previous visits.

"Oh, it's all right," Lenny said. He remained standing, seemingly reluctant to linger. "I'll have to let it go, I guess. I don't have the money for it."

That explained things, Roger thought. He had been quarreling with his lady friend over the money, which she had presumably refused. No doubt that was where he had been last night, and why he had been so late in returning the car.

"I'm sorry to hear that," Roger said, glad that he had not been, after all, the real cause of Lenny's bad humor. "I know you must be disappointed."

"Yeah." Lenny shrugged it off. "I guess I had better be going."

"Oh, but I thought you were going to stay for a while," Roger said. He reached impulsively for the young man, putting a hand on the slim waist. To his amazement, Lenny frowned and pulled away from his touch.

"No, I don't think so, thanks," he said. Without offering any further explanation, he stepped past Roger and into the hall. Confused and disappointed, Roger hurried after him.

"Perhaps we could make it another time?" Roger offered breathlessly, trying to delay the departure.

"Sure, I'll come by sometimes," Lenny said without pausing. He let himself out. "See you," he called as he pulled the door shut, leaving an astonished Roger standing alone in the hall.

It was not until he had returned to the parlor and poured himself a glass of sherry to calm his nerves that Roger remembered the car. He jumped up and hurried to the window. Yes, it was there, sitting in the driveway.

"I'd better put it away," he said aloud, annoyed that Lenny had not even bothered to perform that courtesy.

Even before he reached the car, he saw the damage. The front fender, which had been in perfect shape before, now sported a huge dent, as though the car had been driven into a pole or some such thing.

Roger stood glowering at the dent. No wonder Lenny had been reluctant to bring the car back. Probably this had occurred soon after he had driven away yesterday, and he had been fearful of the reaction when the damage was discovered. One would think, though, that he would at least have mentioned it.

In fact, Roger thought, stepping back to survey the car more fully, the Packard gave every evidence of having been treated rather poorly. It was dirty and splashed with mud. Inside, he found a cigarette burn on the front seat, and the gas tank was nearly empty. He was sure it had been full the day before.

He ran a hand wearily through his hair. Cleaning the car up was no great problem, of course, and he could not object too much to the loss of the gasoline, but the seat would have to be repaired, and the fender, even before he could try again to sell the car.

Maybe his insurance would cover the damage. He wasn't certain. Even so, it meant delay, and the bother of giving the insurance company some sort of explanation. He could tell them the truth, that he had let someone take it to show their mechanic, but then no doubt they would want to investigate, and that could lead to further problems. The only thing he could do was to tell them that he had caused the damage himself, and that made him seem extremely careless.

In the long run, perhaps it would be better to take care of the damage himself. He could call Lenny and complain, of course, but he rather doubted that the young man would offer any compensation.

All things considered, he told himself, starting up the car and driving it into the garage, I may have gotten off lightly. Lenny was obviously not a very responsible person. He might have wrecked the car altogether, and then where would I be?

All in all, he was rather glad to be done with the whole business. The next time, he decided, he would be less friendly toward Lenny. After all these years, he certainly did not want to start courting a lot of trouble.

* * * * * * *

If the brief adventure with Lenny accomplished nothing else, it at least seemed to have dissipated Roger's lethargy. For the following two days, he devoted himself to his work with renewed vigor and greater concentration than he had been able to muster previously.

As for the car, he decided that he did not, after all, have to sell it before the trip. He could just as easily leave it stored and take care of selling it when he returned. By then, maybe he would have thought of some logical way of explaining the damage to the insurance company.

There was still a great deal to get accomplished, however. There was the packing to do, preparations to be concluded for the trip itself, and countless such details. In addition, there was the May Ball, the city's biggest social event.

For almost one hundred years now, the Caldwells had always presided over the ball. Roger himself had been the host for the past fifteen years, and he was scheduled to play that role again this year. It was among the few truly prestigious chores that the family still managed, and although in truth his finances no longer lent themselves to this sort of generosity, Roger was reluctant to abandon the habit.

Probably next year, he thought, they would have to decline, and then of course everyone would know it was because they could not afford it, and they would be the object of jokes. But that was next year, and for this year, at least, he was still very much involved in the preparations.

Two days passed before he saw Lenny again. When he did, it came as quite a surprise to him. At first, after the business with the car, he had wondered about Lenny, and worried slightly about the fact that he had been in the least indiscreet with someone who, it now seemed, was not a very trustworthy sort. Since then, however, he had managed to lose himself in his various tasks and had all but forgotten the dark, handsome youth.

It was one of those quiet evenings, with dinner out of the way and a bit of time simply to relax before retiring. Roger had seated himself with a brandy, and he switched on the radio to listen to some music, when the doorbell rang.

"Who could that be?" he wondered, tempted to ignore the summons. He was expecting no one, and was not really in the mood for any surprise visitor. When the bell rang a second time, however, he acquiesced and rose from his chair to make his way to the door.

"Hello," Lenny greeted him with his most dazzling smile, and in as natural a manner as though he was in the habit of stopping by here unannounced.

"Why, it's you," Roger said. His first reaction, after his surprise, was one of annoyance, but then, immediately afterward, it occurred to him that maybe Lenny had come to apologize about the car, or even to make amends.

"What is it?" he asked, not coldly, but without any great warmth either.

"You don't seem very happy to see me," Lenny said. He did an exaggerated pout.

"Well, to be quite honest, I'm not sure if I should be," Roger said.

"Aren't you going to invite me in? I feel a little unwelcome standing out here in the dark."

Roger yielded, although not without misgivings. "I suppose so," he said, stepping aside, "But I'll expect some sort of explanation."

To his further surprise, Lenny reached down and picked up a suitcase, which he carried in with him.

"What on earth is that?" Roger asked.

Lenny glanced down at the case in his hand. "It's a suitcase. What does it look like?"

"I can see that, but what's in it? What's it for?"

Lenny sighed, as though quite bored with the conversation. "My clothes are in it. What would you expect?"

"Oh, I see. Then you're leaving for somewhere—New York? I believe that's where you told me you were going originally."

"I was, but I can't very well go there, without any money. I lost my apartment."

"I see." Roger did not really see at all. No doubt that lady friend had grown tired of paying the bills for her young lover. Perhaps Lenny had borrowed her car too and had been negligent with it, but he did not see what all this had to do with him.

"Then you won't mind putting me up for a day or two?" Lenny gave him another smile.

Roger did understand then, with a shock. "Oh, no, I can't," he said quickly, "It's quite out of the question."

"But you've got to let me stay. I don't have anywhere to go, and no money." Lenny's tone now was pleading, quite unlike his usually aggressive manner.

"Unfortunately, I'm not in the position to put up house guests," Roger insisted. "At any rate, after the damage you did to my car, you could hardly expect a very warm welcome here."

"Yeah, I felt bad about that," Lenny admitted, looking sheepish, "But I didn't think you were the sort to hold a grudge against a friend. Anyway, it's only for a day or two. I've got a job staring in a few days, and after that I can get out on my own again."

Roger was almost speechless, astonished by the young man's audacity. He had never known anyone quite so presumptuous in his entire life. "Even so," he said, "It's still out of the question. In the first place, how would it look, my moving a strange young man into the house?"

"You could tell everyone I'm your new house boy," Lenny said. "Or a relative, even."

"And how am I to convince my mother, if she calls, that you are a relative? She would be sure to find out about your presence here, and you can well understand that she would be quite upset."

Lenny gave him a shrewd look. His manner changed again, with mercurial swiftness, from a shy, pleading young man to someone cool and determined. "Well, why don't we ask her about it?" he said.

"I beg your pardon?"

"I said, why don't we ask her about it. I'm sure if I talked to your Mama, I could make her understand. Why don't we give her a call right now?" He smiled and looked over Roger's shoulder, to the telephone.

"I will not," Roger said firmly. He moved to block the way to the phone.

"If you don't, I will." This was delivered with the same smile, but it was no longer a pleasant smile.

Roger felt a tremor of fear as he realized that he was being threatened—but what was he to do? If he called his visitor's bluff, would he carry out his threat? Did he even know how to find mother? Of course, that probably wouldn't be too difficult. They were Caldwells, after all.

"Perhaps you had better have a drink," he said weakly, indicating the parlor, "And we can talk this all over."

"I could use a drink," Lenny agreed, setting the case down in the hall. "But there isn't much to talk over. I don't have any place else to go, you see, so I have no choice but to stay here. It would be much more pleasant if you were friendly about it. After all, if we're going to be living under the same roof, we should try to get along."

"This is—this is all so sudden, I don't know what to say." Roger poured a brandy for his guest, and refilled his own glass.

"I don't know why you should suddenly act like you don't like me," Lenny said, taking the drink from him. "I like you. I told you that. I think you're great. All I want is to be friends, okay?"

"And if I decline your offer of friendship, insist that you leave, you'll cause trouble for me, is what you're saying."

"You make it sound so unpleasant. I don't want to be unpleasant, not with you."

Roger saw that he had no real alternative. He was quite certain now that Lenny would indeed follow through on his implied threat. Really, even that was not necessary. He could hardly force Lenny to leave if the young man refused, and to call the police would likewise cause a scandal. Either way, Mother would learn of all this, and the shock might be more than she could bear. For the moment, it seemed that he had no choice but to allow this hard and calculating young man to stay here in the house.

"You say it's only for a day or so?" He did not want to give in too easily.

Lenny's face brightened. "Sure, that's all. Like I said, I've got a job starting in a couple of days, and then I'll be out of here."

"I suppose it can't hurt anything," Roger said with a sigh. "But you will have to leave by the end of the week. There's too much risk that someone will find out you're here."

"Great." Lenny downed the brandy in one gulp. "Where do I bed down?"

Roger had to think for a moment. "Most of the rooms have been closed up for ages. I think the East room would be the most suitable. I'll show you."

He led the way up the wide staircase, his mind crowded full of worries. Two days—but Lenny's commitments to time were not, as he had learned before, very dependable. If he stayed much longer than that, his presence in the house was sure to become known, but what could he do? For the moment, he was at Lenny's mercy. Later, perhaps, he could think of some solution, but just now it seemed wisest and safest to yield.

"This is it," he said, opening the door. The furniture had been covered already. He lifted the cover from a Queen Anne chair. "The furniture will have to be uncovered, of course, but I think you will be comfortable here."

"Nice." Lenny looked around approvingly as Roger uncovered the rest of the furniture. "Bathroom?"

Roger wordlessly indicated a door leading from the bedroom. Lenny opened it and looked over the bathroom briefly. When he returned, Roger had finished with the furniture. He stood with the bundle of sheets in his arms, feeling suddenly like a housemaid in his own home.

"I'll see you in the morning, then," he said. There seemed little that he could say or do at this point.

"Sure," Lenny replied, without even looking in his direction.

Having been clearly dismissed, Roger left and walked slowly down the hall to his own bedroom. He had a sense of being caught up in the pull of a vast tide, drawn helplessly into a vortex that would suck him down to some unknown but terrible end.

Lenny—he had seemed so nice at their first meeting, even on his second visit, with its sexual episode. How had they arrived at this situation? He was virtually a servant in his own home, slave to Lenny's wishes and commands, when by all rights exactly the opposite should have been true.

His mind went back to his childhood, to a day when he had been taken to the zoo. He had been thrilled and awed, as any child is, by the variety of strange creatures, but he had been particularly fascinated and frightened by the reptile exhibits.

He remembered staring in grim wonder at what he had been informed was a coral snake, a tiny and harmless looking creature. It was colored in bands of red and black and yellow, gemlike colors that might have been the design of some master artist, but their stunning beauty only disguised their deadly nature, a fatal sting done up in Christmas wrappings.

Dressed for bed in blue silk pajamas, Roger stood at the window and stared out at the darkness, trying to decide upon some course of action. The light from Lenny's window fell across the lawn below. Roger had a vision of his "guest" as he must be by this time, ready for bed also. He thought of their sexual experience. Did Lenny expect to have that desire catered to also? Frightening though the young man might be, Roger could not deny the thrill it had been to hold that firm young cock, to have it in his mouth. Even its memory served to rouse him now, making his groin tingle.

I should be entitled to some reward, shouldn't I, he thought with a faint smile? Moving from the window, he donned his robe and slipped quietly from his room, returning down the hall to Lenny's closed door, where he knocked softly.

The door opened after a pause. Lenny stood in the opening stark naked. Roger realized with some surprise that, although he had engaged in sex with his visitor, he had not seen him in the nude before. It was a splendid sight. Lenny's shoulders were broad and his chest full and powerful, brushed with the faintest wisps of fine dark hair. At his slim waist, another wisp of hair trailed its way downward over a rippling abdomen, to blossom suddenly in full luxuriance about the splendid flesh that Roger remembered so clearly.

There was little doubt that Lenny was fully aware of his male beauty. He smiled as he stood framed in the doorway, arms braced against the wood, the sculptured columns of his legs bent slightly in a naturally graceful pose.

"What's up?" he asked.

Roger felt suddenly shy in the face of such physical perfection. He blushed and managed to stammer, "I wondered if there was anything else you wanted...?" How stupid, he thought, just like a chambermaid in some Victorian erotica. *Will there be anything more, sir?*

Lenny's smile deepened with cruel amusement. He shook his head lazily. 'Not a thing, thanks," he replied firmly. One hand went to his crotch, scratching with feigned nonchalance that only added to Roger's desire, and his frustration. His eyes were drawn to the area almost against his will. Lenny's hand moved slowly, pointedly.

"Not a thing," Lenny repeated, running his thumb over the deep red crest. He moved back slightly, swinging the door closed. Roger was left alone and feeling foolish in the hall as the door shut in his face.

CHAPTER FOUR

"Are you all right, Mr. Caldwell?"

It was several seconds before Roger was even aware of the voice, or the question it had asked. When he grasped the meaning of the words, he jerked upright in his chair, suddenly alert again.

"Oh, yes," he assured the speaker, embarrassed to discover that the others were all staring at him. "I'm afraid my mind was elsewhere for the moment."

'I see." Mrs. Adams gave him the benefit of a smile that was tactfully disapproving, and glanced again at her notes. "I asked if there were any further questions regarding the preparations."

"No, none at all," Roger said, "I'm fully convinced it will be the loveliest May Ball we've ever done. Thanks, mostly, to your efforts."

"Thank you, that's very kind." The compliment did not seem, however, to compensate for his previous rudeness in failing to give the lady his undivided attention. She turned to the others in the room, a handful of the city's finest society. "Anyone else?"

There was a general shaking of heads and a murmur of negative replies. "Well, then, I suppose that concludes our business for today," Mrs. Adams said. "May I remind you, ladies and Mr. Caldwell, that we have only two weeks before the ball itself. I trust that everyone will see to their little assignments."

Roger was almost surprised to realize that the meeting was over. It had seemed such a brief one. He glanced at his watch, to discover that he had actually been here an hour and a half. So absorbed had he been in his own thoughts that he had been all but unaware of the committee meeting.

"Mr. Caldwell." Chairwoman Adams' voice stopped him just before he reached the door. Roger paused and turned to wait for her.

"I don't mean to pry," she said as she joined him, still struggling to stuff her papers into a small briefcase that had plainly been designed more for style than for utilitarian value. "But I must confess, I've been a little worried about you. Are you sure you're feeling well?"

"Why, yes, of course," Roger said. "A little tired, perhaps, with all that I've been trying to get accomplished. The ball, of course, and closing up the house, and preparing for my trip. It's been more work than I would have imagined."

They walked together through the lobby of the hotel where the meeting had taken place.

"If you're quite sure...." Mrs. Adams sounded actually disappointed. "You understand, of course, that if you don't feel up to hosting the ball, we can certainly make other arrangements. I know how disappointed everyone would be to have anyone but you filling the role, but one must think of one's health. I'm most certain that my son would take your place if it's necessary."

"No, that won't be necessary," he assured her, "You needn't worry. I'll be there as usual."

"I see." Mrs. Adams could not quite hide her disappointment. "Fine, then. I'll see you next week." They had reached the front door. She gave him another of her unpleasant smiles and walked away from him.

Roger nodded to the doorman to have his car brought around. He had no doubt that Mrs. Adams would be only too happy to have her son take his place. After all, they were virtually the city's leading family by now, leaders of the new aristocracy that over the recent years had been carefully replacing those of his class.

Next year," he thought stubbornly as he tipped the doorman and climbed into the Packard, frowning at the sight of the dented fender. Next year, Mrs. Adams, the Caldwells will step aside and leave you entirely free to advance your own position.

The sight of the fender, however, had brought his thoughts back to their original channel, the problem that faced him at home. It had been a full week now since that evening when he had opened the door to find Lenny there with his suitcase to hand. A full week, and his guest was still very much in attendance, nor was there any indication that he intended to depart soon.

Roger had heard nothing more about the "job" that had allegedly been looming on the horizon, nor did Lenny seem to be making any effort to obtain that one or any other job.

There was some consolation in the fact that the week had been largely an uneventful one. It had been partially because of that atmosphere of calm that he had hesitated to question Lenny about his plans. It had been an ominous quiet, brooding and seeming to hint that beneath the surface, troublesome matters were brewing, waiting for the right word or gesture to call them forth.

It had been, as well, a period of considerable frustration for Roger. In his own peculiar way, Lenny had been pleasant enough. There had even been times when, engaged in light conversation, or over one of the meals Roger prepared for them, Lenny seemed actually to be the charming young man he had been on their first meeting. He might almost have been a legitimate houseguest.

Even during those times, however, Roger remained uneasy. He could not help the feeling that he was being toyed with, that secretly Lenny was amused by the situation that he controlled to a great extent. He seemed to derive pleasure from dominating his host, as though he were testing his strength. With each day he grew slightly bolder in his demands, asking for more and more service, and as he found his requests uncontested, he applied new and stricter tests.

In the matter of sex, too, he amused himself at Roger's expense. Each day, Roger was allowed a brief period to see the desirable young creature unclothed, posing and parading about, deliberately provocative in look and gesture. If Roger did not come by his room at night, Lenny found some excuse for stopping by Roger's room briefly, making the way down the hall completely stripped, his glorious cock swinging from side to side as he walked.

During the rest of the day, he utilized every means of stimulating Roger's interest. He would sit across from Roger while they talked, and all the time his hands stroked or rubbed the lengthening bulge at his crotch. He would ask Roger to massage him, even requesting that his buttocks or the back of his legs be kneaded thoroughly.

Once, he complained that the zipper on his trousers was stuck, and insisted that Roger fix it for him. Through the opening, Roger had a limited view of the smooth flesh and dark hair, not unlike the view he had had during their one sexual adventure, and it was with trembling hands that he had managed to operate the zipper, which proved after all to be operating quite normally.

Yet for all the teasing and provocation, there had been no actual sex. On numerous occasions, thinking that Lenny was hinting at that, Roger had made timid advances, only to have them rebuffed, always with the same sense of malicious amusement.

Each time, Roger would vow that he would restrain himself in the future, that he would not afford Lenny any more of that peculiar satisfaction—but the more he attempted to ignore Lenny's overtures, the more insistent those overtures became, until he would again weaken and go for the bait, only to have it once again withdrawn firmly.

Where was it all leading? He knew that Lenny's presence in the house must soon become conspicuous. No one had yet indicated that they knew he was there, but surely that fact would become apparent to outsiders. There was the delivery from the market, for one thing. His order had of necessity increased considerably. Lenny ate and drank heartily.

Lenny spent most of his time in the house, but once or twice he had gone out, offering no explanation. People were certain to see him coming and going.

I'll have to ask him to leave, Roger thought resolutely as he slowed to make the turn into the driveway. As to what he would do if Lenny refused, he had no idea. Probably he would just have to be firm. Lenny was not without intelligence, after all, and surely he could be made to understand that the present situation could not go on indefinitely, without creating a multitude of problems.

Of course, at its worst, the situation was only temporary. In a few more weeks, he would be leaving anyway, closing up the house, and Lenny would have no alternative but to leave. That, however, was still weeks away and he did not relish continuing matters until that time.

There was no sign of Lenny when he entered the house. Roger wondered if he had gone out. Perhaps he really was looking for a job. Maybe I'm worrying over nothing, Roger thought, but without much conviction. He looked over the mail that had come, seeing nothing of any particular importance, and went into the parlor and poured himself a glass of sherry.

He was drinking more these days than was his custom. It was so hard for him to relax. He seated himself in his favorite chair, closing his eyes and rubbing one temple for a moment.

Something about the room bothered him, something that was out of the ordinary. He opened his eyes and frowned, trying to put his finger on the discordant note. His eyes moved slowly and carefully about the room.

The clock, that was it, the mantle clock. It was missing. Lenny must have moved it from the mantle for some reason. He remembered that Lenny had been fascinated by the clock when he had first come to the house.

The clock, however, was not in the room. Roger even got up from his chair and walked back and forth, looking all about him for some sign of the clock, but it was nowhere to be seen.

There was still a faint marking in the dust on the mantle to show where the clock had stood. He thought about the Packard, and the dents in the fender. Could the clock have somehow been broken? He knelt running his fingers over the surface of the carpet, feeling for any broken pieces, and finding none.

"Are you praying?" Lenny asked from behind him. "Or is this some sort of game you're planning for my entertainment?"

Roger jumped at the sound of the voice and turned to see Lenny standing just inside the room. "I didn't hear you," he stammered, struggling awkwardly to his feet.

"I'm not surprised. You looked so engrossed in whatever you were doing." Lenny's voice had a cutting edge to it today—a sign, Roger had already learned, that he was not in a good humor.

"I was looking for the clock."

"On the floor?" Lenny cocked an eyebrow.

Roger felt his face redden, and his own temper flared briefly. "As you can see, it's not on the mantle, where it has always stood. I had no idea where you might have put it, but frankly, I should like to know."

Lenny shrugged his shoulder and turned away, dropping heavily into a chair. "Afraid I can't help you," he said. "I have no idea what clock you're talking about."

"That's ridiculous. You've admired it before. We discussed it one evening. It's been in my family for generations and it's of considerable personal value to me."

"Oh, that clock," Lenny said. "No, I'm sorry, I haven't seen it."

"But you must have. It was here earlier and it's gone now. I'm certain that it did not climb down from the mantle of its own accord and hide itself from me."

Lenny had picked up a book to thumb through the pages. Now, in a sudden gesture, he flung it across the room and jumped abruptly to his feet.

"Look, damn it, are you accusing me of stealing your frigging clock? What the hell would I want with some old clock?"

Roger jumped back, startled from his temper by the display of violent fury. He half expected Lenny to leap across the room and throttle him.

"No," he stammered, his hands fluttering nervously, "It's just that, something's happened to it, that's all, and I'd like to know where it is."

"Why don't you look up your ass? That's where I would like to shove it," Lenny shouted as he strode angrily from the room, in the direction of the kitchen.

Roger stood helplessly silent, afraid of pursuing the subject further, yet unable to dismiss the matter from his mind. The clock was of some value, but more importantly, it was a family possession, something that mattered to him personally. Lenny must know about the clock. It couldn't have just disappeared, and there were only the two of them in the house. Perhaps if he waited until Lenny were in a better humor—he would go to him tonight, in his room, and ask about it again.

The thought of Lenny's room brought a glimmer of hope into his mind. Lenny had admired the clock previously. Perhaps he had simply carried it up to his room, and afterward was ashamed to admit the fact.

Roger stepped into the hall. Lenny was still in the kitchen, probably drinking a beer. Stealthily, although he was in his own home, Roger made his way up the stairs. The door to Lenny's room was closed, as usual, but it was not locked. Unable to overcome a feeling of guilt, Roger nonetheless entered the room.

There was no clock there, either. Feeling disappointed and a trifle ashamed of his actions, he had turned to go when he saw a slip of paper on the dresser, and instinctively picked it up.

It was not something with which he was familiar, and not until he had looked at it for a moment did he recognize it as a pawn ticket—and it had today's date on it.

Before he could think further, he heard a step behind him, and turned to meet Lenny's cold, hard gaze. He knew, when he saw Lenny's face, that his guess had been correct.

"You did take the clock," he said aloud, holding out the pawn ticket. "You took it and pawned it."

For a moment he feared Lenny might strike him. Then, apparently tiring of the scene, Lenny relaxed slightly and shrugged again, walking past Roger to throw himself down upon the bed. "Sure, I pawned the clock," he said, "So what's the big deal? I needed some cash, okay?"

"But it was my clock," Roger said. "This is theft." The casual attitude in which Lenny delivered his confession bewildered Roger more than the deed itself.

"I told you, I needed some money," Lenny repeated, the anger returning to his voice.

"But you can't just take someone else's thing, and sell them. It was an heirloom, it belonged to me, to my family."

Lenny gave an exasperated groan. "I don't know what you're so fired up about," he said. "Look, if you're so worried about the clock, all you have to do is take that ticket down to the pawnshop and pick it up. It's that simple. So quit bugging me about it, okay?"

Roger stared at him dumbfounded. All he had to do was to take the ticket to the pawnshop and buy back his own clock. It was preposterous. The man was mad.

He opened his mouth to protest, but the look on Lenny's face frightened him. He had the impression of a wild, terrifying force about to explode. He suddenly knew that this was a man capable of violence, and he looked now as though he were on the brink of it.

"I see," he said simply. His fingers closed over the paper, clenching it in his fist. There was no answer and, holding his emotions in check, Roger turned and left the room. He was halfway down the hall when the door to Lenny's bedroom was slammed violently.

He would have to go for the clock, of course. It was criminal, but he did not want to lose the piece.

Suppose he did, however, and suppose Lenny decided he needed cash again, for whatever purpose? Why, the clock would just disappear all over again, or maybe something else. For all he knew, it wasn't only the clock. It seemed, as his eyes darted about, that the furnishings of the house were dwindling before his very eyes.

What else, he thought frantically, what next?

CHAPTER FIVE

What had begun as annoyance and apprehension had grown within Roger until it had assumed the proportions of genuine fear. It was not a pleasant state of affairs to admit to oneself, but he was truly afraid of his houseguest.

The incident with the clock had finally revealed to him what should have been obvious long before, that Lenny was a man totally without conscience. He would stop at nothing to further his own selfish ends. In Roger he had found a perfect haven for himself—a comfortable home and good food, with no investment in energy or money necessary on his part. That Lenny would not easily give up such a soft life, Roger was now fully aware. Somehow, he had to persuade or force the young man to leave the house, and Roger's life—but how, without risking retaliation of heaven only knew what sort. It was no longer simply scandal of which he was fearful, but the prospect of physical violence.

The quandary haunted Roger hour by hour as the days passed. He redeemed the clock at the pawn shop, outraged by the amount that it cost him to buy back his own possession, and he returned it to its place on the mantle. Each time that he returned to the house after being out, he went directly to the parlor to see that the clock was still there, fully expecting that Lenny would again make use of this means of easy money.

As it turned out, however, it was not the clock that attracted Lenny's interest on the next occasion, but rather a crystal decanter set mounted in a case of Georgian silver. It was not, as the clock was, on display, and in fact Roger might not have missed it for months, even years. But if Lenny persisted in making his fortune at Roger's expense, he seemed to have decided to make no further secret of the fact, for this time the pawn ticket was left atop Roger's dresser, brazenly conspicuous.

Roger's immediate reaction was one of considerable anger, and he stormed down the hall in the direction of Lenny's room. He halted before he reached the door, however, reconsidering his actions. His righteous indignation would produce no better results, he was sure, than it had with the incident of the clock. No, he would have to find some way of stopping this looting of the house, but facing Lenny and charging him with what was obvious fact was not the answer.

What is the answer, then, he thought anxiously? He was as ill equipped to cope with this situation as he had been to cope with the young man in New York years before, except to pay and suffer the humiliation.

This wasn't a matter of shelling out some cash and leaving the incident behind, however. This was here and now, and a continuing matter. Unless he could find some way to break this chain of events, it would go on and on, until his resources were spent, his nerves exhausted, his name ruined.

"I'll call Courtney," he thought in a burst of inspiration, brightening at the prospect. Courtney Wills, their clever young attorney—there never was a problem that Courtney could not solve for them. He seemed always to know exactly the best thing to do. "He should have been a Caldwell," Roger had said often in the past.

"No, I'll go seen him," he decided instead. That thought was quickly transformed into action. He changed quickly and, without bothering to inform Lenny that he was going out, a courtesy they had ceased to observe, Roger made his way downtown. He was almost to the Talbot Building before he remembered that Courtney was in his new offices now, in a sleek, multi-storied building. Roger changed directions and headed toward that one instead.

"Monstrous edifice," he grumbled to himself as he pulled into the basement garage. Like driving into the mouth of a prehistoric monster. He for one had much preferred the older, more staid Talbot Building, with its valet parking, but then, that was one of the ways in which clever young men like Courtney Wills differed from the Caldwells. For himself, he did not think a business seemed as well run in a modern building as it did in something Georgian or even classical.

The thought of turning his problems over to someone else, particularly someone as capable and shrewd as Courtney Wills, had caused a state of carefree happiness to descend over Roger. Now, however, as he soared upward in the silent elevator, the modernity of the building seemed to emphasize the gulf that existed between himself and the young attorney. His elation began to fade slightly as he tried to imagine just how he should present his problem to Courtney. He could hardly tell him the entire story. Courtney would certainly be less than pleased to learn that his client was a homosexual, and an indiscreet one as well. Under the circumstances, Courtney might very well tell him he had gotten exactly what he deserved.

How then was he to explain the presence of Lenny in the house? He could, of course, merely state that Lenny had come about the car, and then had returned with the expressed intention of staying, but that was more than a little questionable and, at the very least, would make Roger sound almost hopelessly stupid. In any case, he could hardly imagine that Lenny would not make the rest of it known.

In fact, Roger realized as the door of the elevator slid open, he had only two possible alternatives: to tell Courtney everything, which he could certainly not do, or to tell him nothing.

The elevator door clicked and glided closed again. Someone on another floor had pushed the button to summon it and so, to a great extent, made Roger's decision for him. He rode to the basement level, where he retrieved his car and started grimly for home.

* * * * * * *

Even as he pulled into the driveway, he could hear the sound of music, coarse, jazzy music. At first he could scarcely believe it was coming from his house. Whatever faults he might have, Lenny was usually rather quiet about the place. Oh, he had laid claim to an outdated floor model radio from the music room and moved that into his bedroom, but he ordinarily played that at a reasonable volume. This racket, however, seemed almost to threaten the windows with shattering.

So bewildered was he by the din from the house that at first Roger did not even notice the car, a battered older Chevrolet, parked in the driveway. He was almost upon it before he became aware of its existence, and braked the Packard sharply.

So that was it. Lenny was entertaining guests, and obviously they were music lovers of a dubious sort. Well, enough is enough, he thought as he climbed from the car. He might have to put up with a great deal from Lenny, but he was certainly not going to have the entire neighborhood scandalized by Lenny's friends, whoever they might be.

It was certainly not difficult to locate them inside the house. He had only to follow the blare of the music to the parlor, where he found Lenny dancing with one of his visitors—if it could be called dancing.

The young man with him was not unattractive in appearance, if a bit on the seedy side. He was, however, effeminate in the extreme. He was short, no more than five three of five four, and slim, a well proportioned body poured into skin tight deck pants of a slightly soiled white, and a brilliantly patterned shirt.

The other guest was nearly an exact opposite, a huge ape of a man reclining on the divan, his dirty

shoes carelessly perched on the lovely silk uphol-
stery fabric. His features were ruggedly chiseled and
ugly almost to the point of being fascinating. His
body was a massive hulk of muscle that looked as
though it possessed unlimited power.

The trio was oblivious to his arrival. Roger
stood for a moment observing the crude, virtually
obscene dance that Lenny and the young blond were
doing, a dance that appeared to be little more than a
travesty of the sexual act. Their bodies bent and
arched, forcing their bulging crotches together, hips
rocking to and fro.

The music came to a pause finally, giving Roger
an opportunity to assert himself without resorting to
screaming. "What is the meaning of this?" he demanded, stepping into the room.

"Hey, it's my buddy, Roger," Lenny greeted
him, turning to notice him for the first time. To
Roger's surprise, Lenny came quickly to him, clap-
ping an arm warmly about his shoulder as though
they were indeed on the closest of terms.

"This is Roger," he announced to the other two.
"The only real sweetheart of my life. And this is
Marty and Zak."

The small blond, Zak, did not so much as walk
over to them as glide, a smile flickering over lips
that were too red to be their own color. "Hey, you're
cute," he said, fluttering his eyelashes.

Lenny gave Roger a hug, and his hand patted
Roger's rump affectionately. "Yeah, ain't he a doll?
He's the greatest."

Roger was flustered by the unexpected show of
attention, particularly from Lenny. Was this more of
the cat-and-mouse amusement of the past, or only a

show for his friends? Or was it because Lenny had obviously had more than his normal quota of drinks? Lenny's eyes were unnaturally bright and his breath reeked of alcohol.

"This music is very loud," Roger managed to say, but the firmness that anger had given his voice was gone, and his statement carried little authority.

"Ah, come on," Lenny coaxed him. "It's just right for dancing. Show him, Zak. Dance with my sweetheart here." Roger was pushed into Zak's arms, and Zak pressed his body tightly against Roger's in an unsettling way, grinding into his groin.

"I'm afraid I don't dance well," Roger tried to protest, but there was no avoiding the insistent rubbing of the lithe body against his cock. The music had changed to a slow, sensuous throbbing that seemed to blend with the beating of Roger's heart.

"Relax, doll," Zak crooned, clinging tightly. His hands stroked Roger's body intimately.

"What he needs is a drink," the one on the sofa said—Roger tried to remember—Marty, was it? Marty suddenly appeared beside the dancing couple, glass in hand. "Here, try this," he said, raising the glass toward Roger.

"No, I don't want any," Roger tried to protest, to no avail. Marty raised the glass to Roger's mouth and tilted it. The liquid spilled down Roger's chin and some of it into his mouth. He gulped, swallowing and choking as the straight liquor burned its way down his throat. The glass went, and returned, and all the while the music drove on and on relentlessly, and the warm body rubbed hotly against the slowly lengthening flesh inside Roger's trousers.

He felt lightheaded, caught up in the debauched mood of the scene, the raw lust that emanated from the others. He knew he was being foolish, that he would regret succumbing to their blandishments, just as he had regretted surrendering to the temptation of Lenny's physical beauty, yet he could not summon up the resistance to ward off their insistent efforts. The liquor made his head swim—or had it been something more than just liquor? His head felt funny, like it had never felt from mere liquor.

He stumbled and he and Zak fell together onto the sofa. Zak was laughing and, incredibly, Roger found himself laughing with him. He fell away from the small blond, gasping for breath. It was so warm in the room, and he was so dizzy.

Lenny hovered over him, friendly and charming in a way he hadn't been since his first visit. He smiled down at Roger and said, "Here, try this."

Roger shook his head at the cigarette Lenny offered. "I don't smoke," he said, but Lenny only thrust the cigarette at him more determinedly.

"Try it anyway," he said, "You'll like this."

It seemed there was no avoiding it. Roger inhaled a couple of times, blowing small puffs of smoke back into the room. It left a sweet, sickish taste in his mouth, but nothing more.

Then, so unobtrusively that he did not know when it started or how, the room seemed to expand, and he to expand with it. He felt suddenly changed, without being able to determine in what manner he had changed. He was suddenly happy, calmer than before, aware of every sight and sound and scent in a way completely new to him.

There was laughter, a great chorus of laughter. Lenny was laughing, and Zak, too, and the ugly one, Marty, and to his surprise, Roger realized that he was laughing with them. He roared with laughter, looking up at them as they passed the cigarette around from one to the other and bellowed with him.

Lenny knelt beside him and kissed Roger's cheek. When Roger looked up again, Marty had opened his trousers, exposing himself. He brandished his erect flesh like a huge club, holding it with his fist and shaking it at the others, and they all laughed until tears streamed down their cheeks.

"Hey, it's a May pole," Zak shrieked. "Let's dance. Let's dance around the big, beautiful pole."

"Come on," Lenny said. He dragged Roger to his feet. They joined hands, Roger and Lenny and Zak, and danced in a circle about Marty, who continued to shake his cock at them.

Somehow, Roger had no idea how or when, they had rid themselves of their clothes. Roger was almost unaware of the transition, until he sudden realized that they were all naked, whirling insanely about the room in a mounting frenzy of animalistic sexuality.

Still laughing and shouting, Roger fell into Marty's arms. He clawed at the hard muscles of Marty's shoulders and chest, and slithered downward, crazed with desire for the sex godhead. He and Marty toppled to the floor and Zak and Lenny fell upon them, forming a heap of writhing, twisting limbs and scorching flesh.

Roger was drowning in a flood of semen, his mouth filled with the rush of it, it seemed to splash

87

and spray across his feverish body in torrents, rivers, crystal droplets that cascaded over him with mystical clarity and beauty, until his own flood poured from him.

He surrendered himself to the sweetness of total relief, wafted upward on a gossamer cloud into an oblivion of lights and colors and strange, never before heard strains of music.

CHAPTER SIX

The descent from Elysium was a crashing downfall, discordant and thundering. The wave that had borne Roger along so thrillingly sent him breaking across the jagged shoreline of reality, spinning and toppling end over end.

He woke to blinding pain and jangling nerves, but the spinning continued. Even his familiar parlor appeared foreign and grotesque to him. He tried to stand, but the effort was too much and he slumped sideways against the divan as a fit of vomiting seized him. It seemed as though he were trying to empty himself of the entire sordid experience. The waves of nausea swept over him with the regularity and the intensity of a climax.

It was over at last. It receded to leave him weak and shaken. He rubbed his forehead against the cool silk and, with an effort, opened his eyes again and attempted to focus them on his surroundings.

Yes, he was really here, in his own parlor, his own home. He looked down at himself. He was as naked as he had remembered, his pale, flabby body seeming to him unsightly and unspeakably obscene in this formal setting.

The others were still there as well. Lenny was sprawled on another sofa, one leg dangling over the side, his long cock relaxed on his leg, his handsome face smiling in his sleep.

The other two were near Roger on the floor. Marty's big boned body sprawled ungracefully, his limbs spread wide, his mouth open. He was snoring deeply. Zak lay on his stomach near Marty, the sensuous curves of his buttocks turned to Roger's view, his face almost in Marty's crotch. One hand still lay limply upon Marty's large cock, as though even in sleep he continued the crazed orgy of the previous evening.

Sleeping as he was now, Zak had an astonishing look of innocence. He seemed incredibly young and untroubled, with his sweet, pretty face and a small youthful body that, in repose, was free of the exaggerated mannerisms that otherwise detracted form his appeal.

Lenny groaned from the sofa and stirred slightly. Roger grimaced and struggled to get to his feet. He didn't want to face them when they awoke. He could scarcely bear himself, let alone them.

He made it to his feet finally and half-walked, half-stumbled to the door. Not until he was on his way up the stairs did he think of his clothing, still strewn about the parlor. With the memory, he again felt self conscious of his nudity, but he did not return for the clothing. It would be there later. For now, he wanted only to get to the safety of his room, to hide himself not only from their knowing eyes but from his own thoughts as well.

His flight was a futile one, though. His thoughts and his shame remained with him, mocking him. He was sick again in his bathroom. Afterward, he showered, standing for a full half hour under the stinging spray, yet when he emerged he felt still as dirty as before. He shaved despondently, nicking his chin twice and, finally dressed, he seated himself in his room to face what had happened.

They were beasts, the three of them, creatures dredged up from some nightmare realm of animal passions and inhuman hungers—and yet, he had stooped as low as they, he had reduced himself to their level of baseness. Was he as terrible as they? Had he lost not only control of the situation that was growing within this house, but of himself as well?

The mirror across the room gave his reflection back to him. He looked gaunt and aged, and incredibly beaten down. "You're a Caldwell," he said aloud, arguing with his reflection. "Can you have forgotten that altogether?"

He would have to face them, of course, just as he would have to return downstairs and attempt to restore order and cleanliness to the place. He no longer fooled himself that he had any authority here. They would stay until they had exhausted themselves of their devilish game. Neither threats nor tears would coerce them to surrender his home back to him, he was sure of that.

Where this blind roller-coaster ride was leading him, where it would end, he could not guess. He could only helplessly follow the course that Lenny had set for him and wait to see what disaster awaited him.

There was yet one source of strength remaining to him, however, one haven of sanity that he did not have to surrender to them. He was a Caldwell, not a very good one, he thought ruefully, but a Caldwell nevertheless, with all the heritage of dignity that the name implied.

He vowed, with all the resolve that he could muster, that never again would he surrender himself to them, and to their naked carnal desires, as he had done last evening. He would yield to their demands, act as their servant if necessary, allow them to run free in this, his family home, but he would cling jealously to his inner dignity, whatever humiliation he suffered outwardly.

He could hear that they were stirring below. Their loud voices, raucous laughter, drifted upward to grate on his already frayed nerves.

Roger stirred, drawing his shoulders back as firmly as he could, and made his way down to the parlor.

"Hey, it's Roger, baby," Zak greeted him as Roger reentered the parlor. The aura of boyish innocence that Zak had worn while he was sleeping had vanished upon waking.

Someone had made coffee and the three of them were seated, still blatantly naked, on the floor, sipping from steaming mugs. They all greeted him with warm grins, but beneath the surface of their pleasantness, he could see the sneering contempt that he had failed to discern before.

They hated him. Yes, even as they had dragged him down in the filthy abyss of yesterday's sexuality, they loathed him and all that he stood for, perhaps even more than he had come to loathe them.

"I'll clean all this up," Roger said, beginning to gather up the debris. He tried to ignore the fact that their eyes were on him.

"Let it go," Marty said. "I got better things for you to do."

Against his will, Roger looked down at the naked body on the floor. Marty had begun slowly to play with himself, his cock already half hard, the broad head gleaming softly in the morning light.

"I'm afraid this has to be done," Roger insisted, forcing his eyes from the sight. He was relieved that he had felt no desire, only a faint stirring of his previous nausea. At least he was not yet completely immersed in their carnality. He could still exercise some control over his lust.

"I said forget about that." Marty's voice had turned angry. "When the big hairy one wants taken care of, he wants taken care of. You ain't gonna insult him by saying you don't like him, are you?"

There was a moment of tense silence, broken at last by Lenny's low laughter. "Marty's gone soft on you, Roger," he said.

Marty laughed too, dispelling the moment of tension. "Not soft, baby, hard. Marty's gone big and hard for Roger." They all three laughed at that.

"Oh, come on," Zak said, scrambling toward Marty. "I can take care of that big old thing as well as anyone."

Marty laughed again, but to Roger's relief he seemed content to let Zak satisfy his urges—this time, anyway, Roger reminded himself grimly. He glanced up from his cleaning efforts to find Lenny's eyes fastened on Marty and Zak. Roger could not read the message in Lenny's expression—lust, perhaps, or amusement, or something far worse.

A shiver went up and down Roger's spine. Something awful was looming closer and closer, he realized, something still too dark and formless to be defined, but something that he felt sure would bring his entire world crashing down about him.

Still shaken, he stood and walked quickly out of the room, fearful that they might call him back. They did not, however, and he made his escape to the kitchen without incident.

How long would it continue, he wondered, this nightmare into which he had fallen? And where was he to get the courage necessary to survive it?

He knew, without even questioning them, that Lenny's friends had come to stay. There was no surprise in the fact that they were still there, nor even in the fact that no one had seen fit to ask his permission, even out of respect for form. Lenny was master here now, and Roger moved among the halls and rooms like a vague shadow, striving to keep himself as inconspicuous as possible.

His only hope was to avoid them as much as possible. If he must suffer their presence, he could at least spare himself their company, and he devoted himself to that goal, confining himself as much as possible to his own room or to the areas of the house they did not often frequent.

They seemed not to mind particularly, apparently content to have full freedom of the house and its facilities at their disposal. Once or twice, when Roger passed by the open door to the parlor, Marty or Zak would call out to him and wave their cocks invitingly, but they did not insist that he join them. Probably, he thought, they were no more eager for his companionship than he was for theirs.

In any case, they spent the greater part of that first day romping about naked together, drinking

STRANGER AT THE DOOR, BY VICTOR J. BANIS

and swearing, dancing to their loud music, and presumably continuing their grotesque sex party. Their second day in the house was much the same, and Roger remained for the most part unmolested.

On the first night, when he had retired early to bed, he was frightened by the sound of footsteps approaching his room. The door opened and he recognized Lenny's tall, statuesque figure outlined in the doorway. Roger pretended to sleep and after staring silently into the room for what seemed an eternity, Lenny had gone.

The second night, Roger locked his door when he went to bed. Again he heard the footsteps, although he could not say if it was Lenny or one of the others. Whoever it was tried the door and, after a pause, tried it again. Roger held his breath in fear, wondering what outburst of spite his action might provoke. After a while, however the footsteps moved away from the door, down the hall, and though he remained awake for a long time, listening, they did not return.

* * * * * * *

He woke in the morning to a bustle of noise and activity outside his window. Slipping into his robe, he stepped to the window and pulled the curtains aside to look down on the lawn. There were two trucks parked in the driveway, although from this viewpoint he could not make out the lettering on the sides of the trucks. Numerous men in work uniforms moved to and from the trucks, disappearing around the side of the house.

Roger went to the other window and looked down at the back yard and the swimming pool. The uniformed men were cleaning the empty pool and servicing the equipment.

What nonsense, he thought angrily. He tossed aside the robe and dressed quickly. The pool had been empty and unused for years, and there was hardly any need to begin servicing it now that the house was about to be closed up. There must surely be some mistake.

"What's going on here?" he demanded in an angry voice as he rounded the corner of the house. The workmen stopped and gave him their surprised attention. One of them, obviously the foreman, stepped forward.

"We're getting the pool ready, like you wanted," he said.

"That's ridiculous," Roger answered, "I don't want the pool ready, or filled, or anything at all done with it."

The man looked even more bewildered. "But your houseboy called us yesterday afternoon," he said, "Told us you wanted it taken care of pronto."

"My houseboy…?"

"What seems to be the problem?' Lenny's voice was soft as it asked the question, yet it seemed to crack like a whip through the stream of conversation. Roger jumped and turned, looking straight into Lenny's stony face.

Lenny, of course—he should have realized that this was their whim. He saw, in Lenny's eyes, the challenge, daring him, warning him. The workmen, too, were all staring at him, waiting for some further word from him.

Roger felt his face turn crimson. "I'm sorry," he stammered, feeling as foolish as he knew he must sound and look. "It must have slipped my mind. Yes, of course, go on with your work."

He knew their eyes were still on him as he made his way, weary and beaten, back to the house. How stupid of him, to have questioned or challenged. This wasn't his house anymore, he was only a guest here. There was no reason to expect them to ask his permission for whatever they chose to do, and no way in which he could hold them in check.

* * * * * * *

"That was a dumb thing to do," Lenny told him angrily when he found him in the kitchen later. "Those workmen thought you'd gone batty. I had to tell them you had been sick for a while, just to get them to go ahead with the work."

"You might at least have told me what you'd done," Roger replied petulantly. "Then I'd have known. I would not have been in such a position."

"I don't see much of you," Lenny said with a smug grin. "I can't spend all my time tracking you down just to explain every little detail to you."

Roger had the growing sensation that he was mad, that he was imagining this entire experience. Perhaps he wasn't really Roger Caldwell. Perhaps this really wasn't his home.

"Your trouble," Lenny was saying, his voice droning on and on through the ringing in Roger's ears, "Is that you don't take any interest in things. You leave everything up to me, running this whole house and looking after your guests."

He was being scolded, like a little boy who had been careless or naughty, and the worst of it was, he felt like he wanted to cry. There were even tears forming in his eyes.

Lenny's tone relented slightly, and his arm went about Roger's shoulders in a surprisingly gentle gesture. "Okay, okay," Lenny told him, "Don't get all upset, baby, Lenny will take care of everything. What you need is rest, lots of rest. Why don't you just go back up to your room and stay in bed today? Lenny will take care of everything, don't you worry."

CHAPTER SEVEN

There seemed no end to the party that Lenny and his friends were throwing. Roger was only half aware of the hordes of people coming and going from the house. On one occasion there seemed to be dozens of them, of both sexes. Sometimes during the day they were clustered naked about the pool, as noisy and rowdy there as they were inside. At other times they occupied the house, turning it into a scene from some surrealistic rendition of Dante's inferno. There was singing and dancing and endless drinking—and sex, without discrimination or any regard for decency.

Roger emerged from the isolation of his room on one occasion to find his three tormentors with a fourth unknown man and a woman, all of them naked, sprawled on the floor of the parlor. As accustomed as he had become to the licentiousness of Lenny and his friends, Roger was nonetheless shocked by this new example of their depravity. He stood in disgust and watched the tableaux, the performers oblivious to his presence.

Sick with remorse, Roger left them. He wanted to see no more, and as the orgies continued, growing in number and intensity and then diminishing, and growing again, he increased his efforts to avoid them, to shut them from his sight.

Yet even as the abandonment seemed to increase, there was a subtle change in the atmosphere. It originated with Lenny and it confused and puzzled Roger even more than the immorality all about him.

Lenny's attitude toward him had changed. There was the increasing authority that Lenny exercised, of course, and surprisingly, in his more sober moments, he actually seemed to assume an air of genuine responsibility. What puzzled Roger the most, though, was his increasing attitude of patronization. He had begun to pay more attention to Roger.

Often during the day he would appear in Roger's room to ask after him, occasionally even to bring him coffee or food, which he no longer seemed to expect Roger to prepare for them. If there was mail, he usually delivered that to Roger's room as well.

It was a strange seesaw relationship that was now developing between them. On one hand, Lenny actually seemed to be assuming the role of a servant. At the same time, though, it was the servant who was master. Roger found it increasingly difficult to retain his perspective. He scarcely knew how he should act toward this puzzling creature who ruled his life. At one moment he felt himself in the clutches of a demon who would not rest until he had destroyed Roger completely. The next moment, however, the concern with which Lenny asked after his health, or scolded Roger for not eating all of his meal, seemed utterly genuine.

It was inevitable that the noise and activities about the house should eventually provoke some response from his neighbors, and Roger was not particularly surprised when the call came from Mrs. Lewiston next door. The Caldwells and the Lewistons had lived side by side for several generations, and while they were far from friendly with one another, they were at least acquainted and bound together by virtue of class. Even so, it was a rare occasion when they had more than fleeting and incidental contact.

The phone rang on one of the occasions when Lenny was in Roger's room. More surprising than the call itself was the fact that, before Roger could even more toward the phone, Lenny had answered it, speaking coolly into the instrument.

"Caldwell residence," Lenny said into the phone and, after a slight pause, "I'll see if he's in."

He turned to Roger, placing a hand over the mouthpiece. "A Mrs. Lewiston. Who is she?"

"The neighbor." Roger felt rather sure he knew the nature of the call. "I'll take it."

Lenny hesitated and Roger realized that it had not been a question of whether he should speak to the caller, but rather whether Lenny would permit him to do so. After a moment, however, Lenny handed him the receiver, but he waited and listened.

"She's doing well, thank you," Roger replied in response to the question about his mother. Mrs. Lewiston was delaying, he thought, trying to find a tactful way of approaching the real reason for her call.

"You have…guests, I notice," she said finally, measuring her words carefully.

"Yes." Roger did not offer any further explanation. He could think of none that would clarify the situation without making it worse.

"I see." Mrs. Lewiston seemed less than enthusiastic about continuing, but when he offered her no help, she summoned her courage to pursue the matter. "I hope you won't think I'm being too presumptuous, but I wonder if I might ask for a little more, well, restraint, if you know what I mean."

Roger looked at Lenny across the receiver. "Yes. We've perhaps been a little exuberant."

"Then you do understand? I don't mean to complain, but the noise has been a little excessive." She sounded relieved to find that he was taking no apparent offense.

"I'll take care of it," Roger assured her. What else could he say? To quarrel with her would only create further annoyance on her part, and perhaps result in considerable difficulty. "And forgive us for being thoughtless."

"Not at all," she said. "I know how young people can be."

He thought he detected a barb in her words. So, she had seen his guests at some time or other during their comings and goings. He could only guess at the conclusion she had drawn.

When the call was ended, he handed the phone wearily to Lenny and rested his head in his hands.

"What's the beef?" Lenny asked impatiently.

"The noise," Roger told him without looking up. "It's been a little excessive."

Lenny snorted derisively. 'You live here, don't you?" he said. "It's your house, isn't it? What's she got to bitch about if you want to have a little fun?"

And that, Roger thought morosely, was that. He might as well try to fly from his window as to try to persuade Lenny that Mrs. Lewiston was right, that the noise was outrageous, that it should be curtailed for the sake of decency. There was no longer any decency in the house.

He glanced up as Lenny, obviously unperturbed by the complaint, started from the room. Lenny had said, "It's your house, isn't it?"

"But it isn't," Roger said.

Lenny stopped and looked back at him. "Huh?" he asked absently.

"Nothing," Roger said with a shake of his head. "I was only talking to myself."

Lenny gave him a queer look. Then he shrugged and went on his way. The day of judgment was drawing nearer and nearer, Roger thought in despair, the dreaded climax that he could not yet even imagine.

* * * * * * *

That climax came closer with the arrival of the monthly bills. The ordinary ones—lights, gas, telephone—were slightly higher, as was to be expected, but it was when he opened the one from the market with which he dealt that he was delivered the real shock.

The food costs, of course, had skyrocketed, but even that expense seemed trivial alongside the hundreds of dollars in charges for the beer and cigarettes the market had delivered to the house. Roger flipped through the receipts. They were duly signed, all of them, by his "houseboy"—Lenny's signature glaring back up at him with the same cold intensity of Lenny's dark eyes.

Roger pressed his fingers against his temples and tried to think of what he should do. He was headed for disaster, he was convinced of it. Even if scandal could be averted, the finances of the Caldwell family, dwindling over the many years, would not long sustain the sort of reckless spending that was becoming increasingly common in the household. He had the pool to consider as well, the bill for which had not yet arrived, and he little doubted that day by day his young guests would hit upon more and more schemes that would drain and, in time, totally deplete his financial resources.

He realized now that there was little likelihood of avoiding the scandal that he so feared. He was fully aware that Mrs. Lewiston's call had done nothing so far as lessening the activities in and about the house, and he little doubted that the lady would register further complaints, perhaps even with the police. It was a fact, too, that Roger's increased spending could not escape note. The accountant who handled their bank accounts for them would eventually question the peculiar expenditures, and Mama was sure to notice them on her monthly statements.

There seemed no escape. Whatever way he turned, Roger could see only tragic ends. Strangely, it was this very hopelessness that gave him finally the courage to make a stand. He had, as he saw it, little to lose. Whatever course of action he pursued, he faced ruin. That being the case, Lenny's hold over him had proven self-defeating.

* * * * * * *

"I want to talk to you," he addressed Lenny when he found him alone in the study. It was one of those rare occasions when the house was relatively quiet. The other two were not in sight, perhaps sleeping somewhere to gather strength for their next carnal outburst.

"What's up?" Lenny gave him only token attention, continuing to doodle on the pad before him on the desk.

"Everything." For once Roger did not feel frightened. He had gone beyond that stage. "I must ask you to leave, you and your friends."

That captured Lenny's full attention finally. He looked up with some surprise and anger that quickly turned into amusement.

"Sometimes your sense of humor really passes me by," he said.

"I wasn't attempting to be humorous. I've gone as far as I can go without...." His voice broke for an instant and he struggled to regain control of it. "I want you to go, that's all. I don't care to argue the matter, or even discuss it, but I must inform you that unless you and your friends are gone by morning. I will have to take action. I know that I will suffer certain consequences for it myself, but I shall have to call the police nonetheless."

"I don't think you will do that," Lenny said.

"Yes." Roger shook his head stubbornly. "Yes, I will do exactly that," he said.

He did not wait for the burst of temper he was sure would come, but turned on his heel and walked rapidly from the room. Not until he was in his own bedroom did he realize how tense he had been. He felt as though he had been holding his breath the entire time.

In the wake of his relief came a sense of jubilation. He had done it. He had taken his stand, drawn the battle lines. He was committed now to holding to his course. It remained only to see what Lenny's move would be. The next step in their drama was up to Lenny.

CHAPTER EIGHT

Whatever consequences were looming as a result of Roger's act of defiance, he noted throughout the day that he had produced one more than welcome change: silence. The house remained ominously still as the day passed slowly, with none of the customary revelry below.

Roger even wondered once or twice if perhaps his guests had gone already, but he dismissed that possibility. He would have seen them leaving, or would certainly have heard them. No, they were still here, and the agony of not knowing what they were planning or doing was almost more uncomfortable than their usual rowdiness.

By late afternoon, Roger could hardly endure the suspense. His courage had begun to pale somewhat as night grew nearer. A simple display of temper on Lenny's part would have been fairly easy to bear, but this, waiting for some reaction that was bound to occur and not knowing what form it would take, was a dreadful experience.

Roger paced his room, pausing once or twice to listen when some sound in the house arrested his attention. Peculiar, he thought grimly, at one time I was perfectly accustomed to the silence of this house and found noise obtrusive. Now, I've grown so accustomed to the noise that the silence is positively unnerving.

At last he could bear it no longer. He left his room, closing the door softly, and moved down the hall quietly. He hesitated outside the closed door to Lenny's room. It was impossible to tell if Lenny were there or not.

"He may be packing," Roger thought hopefully, although without much confidence. Not particularly eager for a confrontation, he moved on without knocking and descended the staircase. There was no one in sight here, either. He checked the parlor, their most frequent gathering place, and found it empty as well.

Still moving stealthily, he started for the kitchen. As he passed along the hall, his eyes were attracted to the console in the hall, to the letters there. It was there that he customarily left his mail, so that he would be certain to notice it when he was going out and could take it with him to drop in the letter box down the street, but he had not written anyone of late and it seemed incongruous to think of Lenny and his friend writing letters.

For a long moment Roger remained where he was, staring in the direction of the white envelopes, suspicions already forming in his mind. Then, slowly and with uncertain movements, he walked to the console and picked the letters up.

They had overlooked almost no one with their correspondence. Roger stared in horror as he flipped through the envelopes: Mama, the local newspapers, his accountant, his attorney—where had they gotten the addresses, he wondered, and immediately an-

108

swered the question for himself. His address book was in his desk in the study, and Lenny had made free use of that room, as he had most of the house.

There was no need to open the letters. He could pretty well guess what they had to say. His first reaction was to destroy them, and he even half tore one of them, but that was a futile gesture, certainly. Lenny would only write others, possibly in even stronger terms.

He imagined the results the letters would produce if they were mailed. By now, he was no longer so frightened by the prospect of a scandal, or the embarrassment that would go with it—but, Mama— a letter of this sort might well be more than her heart would bear. The shock, and the threat of social ruin, would probably kill her.

Lenny had won, of course. Roger could not stand up to that threat. Carrying the letters with him, he mounted the stairs again. He paused at Lenny's door and without knocking, opened it and stepped in. Lenny was sitting up in bed, reading. He lowered the magazine to his lap and stared expressionlessly at Roger. His eyes dropped to the letters in Roger's hand and came back to Roger's face again, and his lips curled in the faintest of smiles.

"These won't be necessary," Roger said simply. He tossed the letters in the direction of the bed. They missed, scattering upon the floor instead. Unable to meet the amused eyes of the young man on the bed, Roger turned despondently, his shoulders drooping, and left, making his way back to his own room.

* * * * * * *

It was the following day when Mr. Brooks from the travel agency called to inform Roger that the preparations were complete for his trip to Europe.

"I could drop everything by your home if you're going to be free," Mr. Brooks suggested.

With all that had happened of late, Roger had completely forgotten the European trip and his visit to Emily. He frowned at the telephone receiver as though disapproving of its reminder.

Before, he had welcomed the prospect of the trip as a solution to the problem of Lenny's presence in the house, assuming that with his departure, Lenny would go on his way.

He no longer considered that likely. If he were to leave, Lenny and his friends were almost certain to remain in residence here, and while he had little authority left to exercise, his presence was certainly better than giving them unrestrained occupation of the premises. He was certain that to leave and turn everything over to them would be ultimately even more disastrous. No, until he could come up with some solution to his problem, he dared not go.

"I'm afraid I'll have to cancel the trip," he informed Mr. Brooks, not without some regret.

Mr. Brooks was appropriately surprised. "But everything is ready," he said, "The reservations are made, the hotels, everything."

"Then I'm afraid they will have to be cancelled," Roger said. "I'll pay you, of course, for your trouble."

"If you're not happy with the arrangements...." Mr. Brooks seemed to regard the cancellation as a personal affront. He sounded not unlike a petulant child whose plans have been thwarted.

"No, it's nothing of that sort. I've had a change of mind, that's all. Perhaps a little later in the season, I can see my way clear to go."

"Reservations are hard to get later in the season."

"I have full confidence in your ability to manage such matters." Roger was firm, and in the end, Mr. Brooks yielded unhappily.

Roger wondered, when the phone conversation was over, how much later he would be able to plan the trip, if at all. Surely the present situation would come to an end eventually, but what end, and when? How far into the future did Lenny's plans extend, or did he consider the future at all? Would he grow bored with his current existence and move on as casually as he had come, or was there some further scheme taking shape in his mind that Roger could not yet fathom?

Later in the day, Mrs. Adams, chairwoman for the May Ball, called. Not until he heard her voice, annoyingly sweet as usual, did Roger realize that he had also forgotten the committee meeting of the day before.

"We missed you yesterday," she said with mock concern. "I hope there's nothing amiss."

"Oh, no. No, I was just a little under the weather," he replied.

"I thought so." There was an unmistakable note of triumph in her voice. "I just knew last week that you weren't feeling well. I suppose you'll be wanting my son to take your place tomorrow night."

Tomorrow night? Was it that soon? Roger had nearly forgotten the ball itself, and his expected presence at it.

"No, that won't be necessary," he said abruptly. "It was only a slight discomfort, and I'm feeling quite well now. Have no fears, I'll be there tomorrow night."

"Oh, well, if you're sure...." Her disappointment was obvious.

Afterward, Roger wondered if indeed he had done the right thing. Surely there could be no harm in leaving the house to Lenny and his cronies for one evening. After all, he often went out and their behavior so far as he knew was no worse for his absence. In any event, it would take a great deal to convince him to shirk his responsibilities regarding the annual festivities—particularly this year, which was sure to be his last one.

No, he would make his appearance as host and sponsor of the affair. It would probably do him good anyway, to get out of the house and mingle with people of a higher quality than his recent companions. There were times when he was beginning to fear that he might, through association, become like them, though that was a difficult end to imagine.

Even the thought of getting out of the house and attending the ball worked on Roger as a tonic. He found his spirits lifted considerably and, during the morning, he busied himself with preparations for the following evening. His formal wear had to come out of storage—thank heaven Mrs. Adams had called or he would never have remembered them in time— and taken to the cleaners for rush service. He would have liked to hire a driver for the Packard, but in view of its damaged fender, he decided instead to travel by taxicab.

He stopped at his barber's for a trim and a manicure, and even splurged on a facial massage, which he was well aware did little for his appearance, but which did wonders for his morale.

By the time he arrived home, he felt better than he had felt in many days. Not even the sight of Lenny, who appeared in the parlor doorway as Roger came down the hallway, could dampen his spirits. Roger gave him a cheerful but curt greeting and went right by him, and up the stairs.

Lenny was not so easily ignored, however. A short time later he appeared at the door of Roger's room. He watched in silence as Roger sorted through his jewelry, deciding what he would wear.

"Going some place?" Lenny asked finally when it became apparent that Roger did not intend to offer an explanation.

"To a social affair," Roger said without looking up. "Nothing you would be interested in."

"Would this be the May Ball, by any chance?" Lenny asked.

Roger did look up at that, surprised. He would hardly have expected someone of Lenny's social status to know of such a prestigious event. "Yes. How did you know about that?"

"I ran across some notes in your desk—committee lists and reports of meetings, things like that."

"I trust you found them interesting," Roger commented dryly. It was exasperating the calmness with which this creature admitted to examining his personal papers.

"Not very." Lenny crossed the room and picked up a ring from Roger's jewel case, examining it briefly. The diamond flickered brilliantly with reflected light.

"I wonder if that's wise," Lenny said, replacing the ring in the jewel case.

"Wise?" Roger had no idea what he meant.

"Your going to that party, I mean," Lenny explained. "You've been going in and out a lot lately. I've been wondering if people won't get suspicious. After all, you have houseguests. People might wonder why you're neglecting them."

"I am confident that you will have some explanation in the event that you are questioned by my friends and associates. An unlikely prospect, I should think."

"I thought you were concerned about what people thought."

"Isn't it a little late for you to think about that?" Roger did not attempt to conceal his bitterness.

"Maybe. Maybe not. Anyway, I think it would be a good idea if you forgot about this ball. In fact, maybe you ought to think about spending more time here at home. We miss you. Just the other night, Zak was saying...."

"I could not care less what Zak was saying," Roger interrupted sharply. "And I can spare you the necessity of pursuing this matter further. I have yielded to your demands on nearly every count, because I felt that it was best to do so. You've seen fit to run my house for me, spend my money, dispose of my possessions and endanger my reputation, but on this subject I intend to be firm. The Caldwells have hosted the May Ball for many years, a fact in

114

which I take a great deal of pride. The Caldwells will host the ball this year as well. You may threaten me in any way you wish. I fully intend to be present when the ball begins. And as for my going in and out of the house, I should like to point out that I am not your prisoner. I shall come and go as I wish, when I wish, where I wish."

Roger's eyes were flashing angrily by the time he had finished and had warmed up to his subject. Lenny said nothing for several minutes, merely staring at Roger in that hard, calculating manner he had.

"I see," he said finally.

Roger breathed more easily. He had expected something more of a fight on this question, and he had been prepared to hold his ground, but now it seemed that would not be necessary. "If you will excuse me," he said in a calmer tone, "I have a great deal to do."

"Of course." To Roger's surprise, Lenny still offered no argument. He seemed, in fact, quite calm and friendly as he left the room.

A victory for me, Roger thought happily, returning his attention to the selection of jewelry.

CHAPTER NINE

It was not long after his scene with Lenny that Roger received yet another call about the Ball. This one came from Mrs. Clark, a kindly woman with whom Roger had been long acquainted, if only slightly, who was chairwoman of the invitation committee.

"Mr. Caldwell, I'm so embarrassed," she said in her breathless fashion that made every conversation sound far more imperative than they usually were.

"Embarrassed?" Roger ordinarily had little to do with the preparing of the invitation lists and, in fact, could not guess the reason for the call, let alone the basis for Mrs. Clark's embarrassment.

"About your nephew, I mean," Mrs. Clark said, but that did nothing to clarify matters in Roger's mind. He did indeed have a nephew, Emily's son, but so far as he knew, Glen—was that even the right name?—was in Zurich. Roger had never been well acquainted with the boy, and knew of him only from Emily's infrequent letters.

"I'm afraid I don't understand," he said.

Mrs. Clark sighed into the phone, obviously reluctant to explain, but feeling it her duty to do so.

"He called me. Oh, I can imagine how awkward it must have been for him, the pour soul."

"He called?" Roger was just beginning, finally, to understand. It was not a pleasant thought.

"Yes, and it's just awful that it should have been necessary at all. I realize you must have mentioned the matter to me, and I won't make excuses. Frankly, it must have totally escaped my mind. I didn't remember a thing about it."

"I see." Roger was hesitant to say more than necessary until he learned more about the call. There was still the possibility of some misunderstanding.

"And I wouldn't blame you in the least for being furious with me."

"Not at all. Things do happen," he said.

Mrs. Clark was clearly relieved. "Well, it's nice of you to look at it that way. Anyway, I've cleared it all up. I sent the invitations to your nephew by messenger—and his traveling companions, too, of course."

"You invited them to the ball?" Roger could hardly believe that even Lenny would have gone this far. There seemed no end to his audacity.

"Yes. I'm really looking forward to seeing him, too. This would be Emily's son, wouldn't it? Do you know, I haven't seen him since he was a baby? He certainly sounded like a fine young man on the phone."

"Yes, he does give that impression," Roger agreed.

"I know how much you must be enjoying his visit. I'm only sorry I nearly spoiled it for him by excluding him from the invitation list, but it's all straightened out now, I'm sure."

"Yes, everything seems to be settled," Roger said.

He barely heard the rest of Mrs. Clark's remarks. Roger's thoughts were on Lenny and the trick he had pulled. How insane! Even if it had worked thus far, and he had managed to obtain invitations to the Ball, Lenny could not for a moment imagine that he could carry off his deception. Mrs. Clark might not have seen Glen since he was a baby, but there would be others at the Ball who had seen him no more than five years ago, on his last visit. They certainly would realize Lenny was an imposter.

I must talk to him, Roger thought anxiously. If only Lenny had discussed the matter with him. If he had known that the Ball mattered so much to him, they might have been able to work something out, perhaps made it possible for Lenny to attend, but not posing as Emily's son.

He found Lenny in the parlor. Lenny gave him a questioning look as Roger entered the room. The drawn look on Roger's face undoubtedly told him that Roger knew what he had done.

"I've just talked to Mrs. Clark," Roger said breathlessly, determined to hold his temper and to reason with Lenny.

"So?" Lenny gave a disinterested shrug.

"She explained to me about the invitation. You realize that this is madness, surely?"

"Why, I thought you'd be pleased," Lenny said with an air of hurt innocence. "If not by my ingenuity, then by the fact that you won't have to go alone. We're going to accompany you, all three of us."

"But you can't," Roger insisted, his voice rising. "They'll know the minute you walk in that you are not my nephew. Don't you see, it just can't be done?"

"But it can, and it will be done," Lenny said. "In fact, we have a little surprise for you."

"Surprise?" Roger did not feel that he was up to any more of Lenny's surprises.

Just then, Marty called from upstairs. "All set," he yelled loudly.

"Fine," Lenny called back. "Bring him on down. Roger, baby, is here. I think he'll get a kick out of this."

"What are you up to?" Roger asked tensely. He had learned to recognize the look that was now on Lenny's face as an omen of impending trouble.

"You'll see in a minute," Lenny said, grinning wickedly. "Wait until Marty and Zak get here."

Roger stared anxiously at the door from the hall, holding his breath. What could they have in mind? Whatever it was, he was certain that he would not find it pleasant.

A moment later, Marty and Zak appeared in the doorway. Marty arrived first, but it was Zak who gave Roger the shock, pausing to pose in the doorway. He wore a scarf tied about his head, and he had made up his face, but in a grotesque manner. He wore an outdated but still splendid gown of red silk, but on him, with his clown's face, it looked ludicrous.

"What the hell?" Roger was aghast. "That dress, it's Mama's. Where did you get it?"

120

"We found it in one of the packing boxes," Zak explained with a shrill laugh. "Isn't it divine?" He waltzed about in a circle, causing the skirt to billow out. "Oh, I'll be the belle of the ball."

"Take that off!" Roger cried angrily. "That's my mother's dress, don't you understand? Have you no decency?"

"Why, Roger." Lenny grabbed Roger's arm in a firm grip and restrained him from rushing at Zak, as he had started to do. "We thought you'd be pleased. I wanted Zak to look lovely for the Ball, and that's the nicest dress we could find in the house. Your mother must have taken her best things with her."

Roger stared at him in disbelief. "The Ball? But you couldn't be considering...you don't mean you intend for him to attend dressed like that? Why, they'd never let you through the door of the place. You must be mad."

"But we'd be with you, Roger," Lenny said in a reasonable voice. "Don't you see, they'll hardly send us away? You're the guest of honor, or something like that, and I am your nephew, and these are my traveling companions, Marty and Lady Zak."

They all laughed aloud at that. Zak screeched and tossed the skirt of the dress into the air, revealing hairy legs and an absence of underwear.

Roger swayed weakly, his vision blurred as tears of frustration filled his eyes. "You can't," he moaned helplessly. "You just can't. It would ruin me, ruin the ball. You must listen to reason."

"Now, now," Lenny said in a scolding voice. "I did listen to reason. You insisted that you had to attend the party, and I gave in to you. It's just that, if you're going, we're going to. Why, that's downright selfish of you not to want to share the fun with us."

It was more than Roger could bear. He began to cry in earnest, his shoulders shaking uncontrollably. He was so helpless against them. Everything he tried to do, they turned into a nightmare. No matter where he turned, they were there before him, blocking his way, mocking him. Their voices filled his head until he thought it must burst from the din.

Lenny's arms were suddenly about him, comforting him as though he were a child. "There, there," Lenny crooned softly. "Don't cry, your Lenny will take care of everything. Come on now, I'll take you upstairs."

Still sobbing, Roger allowed himself to be steered form the room and up the stairs. As they climbed, Lenny continued to comfort him with words.

"You haven't been feeling well lately, you poor baby," he said sweetly. "You've been running around too much, for one thing, and not getting enough rest. And something's been bothering you, I can tell."

Roger's sobs rose in volume. He must be insane, he must be imagining this Alice-in-Wonderland experience.

"Lenny will take care of everything, don't you worry. We'll call that woman back, Mrs. Adams, and we'll just explain to her that you can't make it tomorrow night. She'll have to get someone else in your place."

"But I want to go," Roger said in a whimper.

"No, now, you know you're not up to it," Lenny said firmly. "We'll have to see that you start taking better care of yourself, you naughty boy."

In Roger's room, Lenny helped Roger into the bed, stretching him out on the soft surface. Roger lay where he was placed, crying softly into the crook of his arm. He heard Lenny dialing the phone, and a moment later, heard him ask for Mrs. Adams.

"It's Mr. Caldwell's houseboy," Lenny explained, sounding to Roger as though he were very far away. "There's been a small problem. I'm afraid Mr. Caldwell won't be able to attend the Ball tomorrow night. Yes, his health. He hasn't been at all well lately."

The voice droned on and on, explaining Roger's failing health. On the bed, Roger found himself almost believing it. Perhaps he really was ill. So much was happening. It was becoming difficult for him to think clearly. Maybe Lenny was right. Maybe it was best that he not attend. Mrs. Adams would be pleased, certainly, and her son would gladly take his place.

I can rest, Roger thought. Strange, he had not realized before just how tired he really was. He felt totally drained and weak, and genuinely in need of rest.

Lenny finished his conversation and hung up the phone. He came back to the bed and, surprisingly, seated himself on the edge near Roger. He stroked Roger's temple gently.

"That's a good baby," he said in his most tender voice, "Just rest, now. Lenny will take care of you. Just leave everything to Lenny, and do what Lenny tells you, and everything will be fine."

"Yes, yes," Roger agreed faintly. He no longer had the strength to disagree. It was easier to yield, to give in to the strength of Lenny's demands.

"And I'll be good to you, too," Lenny said. He took Roger's hand and moved it to his lap. Roger's hand jerked away as it touched bare flesh.

"No, no," he whimpered. Not that, he didn't want sex, not with Lenny, not now, not ever.

"Come on," Lenny was insistent. One hand lifted Roger's head from the pillow and turned it toward him. "You know you like this big, fat worm, baby. And it'll make you feel better, like medicine."

Roger wanted to protest, but he felt the press of warm, rigid flesh against his lips. He tried to draw away, but his head was held firmly in place. His lips parted, yielding to the insistent flesh, as it slid full into his mouth, against his tongue.

"That's a good boy," Lenny whispered. He began to move to and fro, the bed creaking slightly. Roger felt the invading column making its way far back into his throat, retreating, then thrusting deeply again—and despite his disgust, he was responding.

So beautiful, he thought, opening his eyes to stare at the naked belly before him, like a beautiful wild animal, dangerous, but exciting, too.

"That's the way," Lenny said. He moved, rolling Roger over and crouching above him. His movements were no longer gentle, but hard, deep lunges into Roger's mouth as his ardor grew. Roger coughed and choked slightly, but the tempo and the intensity of Lenny's thrusting only increased.

"You're good at this," Lenny said hoarsely, "So nice to Lenny's big, fat worm. Lenny will take care of you, don't worry. Be nice to Lenny's cock, baby, chew away."

Roger hated himself for this, for enjoying what was happening, and yet he found his hands lifting upward to cling to the powerful, thrusting hips. He welcomed the attack, and when it reached its zenith, erupting hotly far back in his throat, he welcomed that spurting flow, too, hungrily and desperately.

He was Lenny's now, conquered completely.

CHAPTER TEN

Roger's spirit was broken, and with it his physical strength seemed to fade as well. He remained in bed as though he truly were ill.

Strangely enough, it was one of the more pleasant experiences of his recent past, and that was due mostly to Lenny. He had again reversed his attitude toward Roger. Now, in place of the hard coldness he had previously shown, he was suddenly all concern and kind attention. He waited upon Roger patiently and efficiently, bringing his meals to him on a tray, massaging his shoulders when Roger commented that they were sore, and in general carefully looking after his needs and wants.

Roger concluded that Lenny had been right on that one point—he did need rest. He had not realized just how tired and run down he had been, but it was truly a relief now to linger in bed, doing nothing and caring for nothing, with all this wonderful attention being lavished upon him.

He still regretted the Ball, but he tried not to think about that, particularly during the day of the event. In this respect, too, Lenny seemed determined to do right by him. During the evening, when Roger would otherwise have been in attendance at the festivities, Lenny came up just to spend some time with him.

The visit was well timed. Roger had been sitting up in bed, imagining the Ball itself, and that he was there. He saw himself dressed and groomed, smiling, nodding, bowing to people he knew, putting across the sort of breeding and graciousness that Mrs. Adams and her boorish son could never accomplish.

In his imagination, he danced, the first dance that would open the evening. He was actually humming a dance melody, his head rolling from side to side, when Lenny came into the room. The fantasy vanished, leaving Roger feeling oddly empty.

"How's it going?" Lenny asked, carrying a tray to the table beside the bed.

"Fine, thank you," Roger said meekly. "What's this?"

"I brought you some hot chocolate. It'll help you to sleep soundly. You had bad dreams last night."

"Did I? I don't remember," Roger said. He wondered how Lenny could know that. Had he come here during the night to watch? It was so unlikely, and yet, Lenny was a man of so many contradictions. Who would ever have thought he could be as sweet and charming as he was right now?

He accepted the cup of chocolate, sipping it slowly. Lenny seated himself on the edge of the bed and lit himself a cigarette. The mood was friendly, relaxed and comfortable. Roger felt more at ease than he had in weeks.

"Marty and Zak asked how you were doing," Lenny said. "They wanted to come up and see you for a bit, but I told them to keep their hairy asses out of here until you were feeling better."

It was even more incredible, Roger thought, to imagine Marty and Zak feeling any concern for anyone other than themselves. Maybe, he told himself, I misjudged them. He found himself relaxing as he sipped the warm chocolate. They had been difficult, true, but maybe that was partially his fault. Perhaps he had not done all he could have done to establish a friendlier relationship.

Lenny was silent for a while, engrossed in his own thought. One hand absentmindedly stroked Roger's groin under the coverlet.

"Ever been to California?" Lenny asked unexpectedly.

"Just twice," Roger replied. "That's been quite a number of years ago, and at that I didn't get to see much of the area. I was there on business, you see. Why do you ask?"

"It's a great place. I really love it. Sunshine and ocean and mountains—and swinging people. It's the place for really living."

"Why did you leave it, then?" Roger asked. "Surely Ohio must be rather dull by comparison."

Lenny laughed softly. "Yeah, it sure is," he said. "I left there because of money, because I didn't have any. That's the catch, you need money to live there, to really live. I mean, if you've got it, you're a king, and if you haven't you're nothing. I'll go back someday, but I'll go back with money." An edge of bitterness had crept into his voice as he spoke, more to himself actually than to Roger.

For a fleeting moment, Roger felt an incredible tenderness toward the young man beside him. He tried to imagine what it must be like, being without money all one's life. It was terrible, he was certain. What bitterness that must produce. It was little wonder that Lenny had his faults.

The moment of tenderness passed, however, and a note of apprehension took its place, as Roger remembered their situation. Money—it was money that had first brought Lenny to this house, and that had kept him here. Money had given rise to the entire situation they were in—not affection or tenderness or friendship, but money, plain and simple.

"What's the matter?" Lenny asked.

Roger jumped slightly. He had been so wrapped up for the moment in his own thoughts that he had forgotten Lenny's presence beside him.

"Nothing," he said, "Why?"

"You made a nasty face there for a moment. Is something wrong with the hot chocolate?" Lenny looked at him with concern.

"No, not at all, it's delicious." Roger suited his actions to his words by finishing off the last of the drink. "I was just remembering something. Nothing important."

Lenny seemed satisfied with the answer. He took the cup away, returning it to the tray, and fluffed up the pillow behind Roger's head. "Okay, that's enough for tonight," he said. "You're supposed to be nice and sleepy by now."

"I am," Roger confessed drowsily. The chocolate had relaxed him completely. His eyelids felt monstrously heavy as he sank down into the pillow. For a moment, Lenny's face hovered overhead, looking down at him. Then it came closer and Lenny's lips brushed his forehead lightly.

"Good night, now," Lenny said, very low.

"Good night," Roger answered. He felt deliciously content, light and carefree, as though he could float up into the clouds. How had he ever been so unhappy, or so torn by fears and conflicts, he wondered? Everything was fine now, wonderful and delightful. He was floating, drifting, drifting....

* * * * * * *

He was spinning wildly, careening through an eternity of blackness shattered by flashes of blinding light. Pain wracked his body as he tumbled and plunged, clawing helplessly for something to cling to, to check his fall.

"Oh, God, God," he moaned, writing and twisting.

"Easy, baby, easy now." The voice, it was familiar, but whose was it, where was it coming from? If only he could focus his senses, get his bearings.

"Gently, that's a boy." Lenny—yes, it was Lenny's voice, cutting through the darkness.

"Lenny!"

"I'm here," Lenny answered his cry, "It's okay now, Lenny will take care of everything. Just relax."

Roger felt hands on him, gentle hands, and the spinning eased. He was returning to reality, slowly, painfully.

"You're okay now, just sleep, you'll be all right," Lenny told him.

Roger slept again, but it was an uneasy flight into the dark abyss. He fell and plunged, and rested, only to spin and thrash about again.

He woke to incredible pain. His head throbbed violently and his throat felt aflame and scorched. At first the ceiling overhead rocked and swayed sickeningly. It slowed finally and, at the same time, the closer blur came into focus. It was Lenny, staring down at him.

"Lenny," he gasped hoarsely, his voice sounding foreign and far away even to his own ears.

"It's okay now," Lenny insisted calmly.

"I've been sick." The nightmare came back to him, the horrible plunge through blackness and the pain.

"Yes. Drink this." Lenny lifted his head and Roger felt the coolness of glass against his lips. He tried to ask what it was, but the glass was insistent, the liquid spilling against his lips, and he drank, welcoming the relief to his parched throat.

"You'll be all right now," Lenny assured him, lowering his head to the pillow again. "Lenny's here, don't worry."

"Yes, Lenny's here, I'm all right now," Roger said. Then he was off again, into the blackness, suffering the agonies of a hundred hells. There were cries—were they his own?—and the lights and the pain, until he thought that he must be beyond life, had died already, was in hell.

* * * * * *

"He's coming around." That was Lenny's voice again. Roger tried to bring his mind together, to collect the scattered fragments of his consciousness.

"Yeah. Hold his arm." Another voice. Marty? Zak? No, this was a voice he didn't know.

His eyes opened at last, reluctantly obeying his brain's orders. Swimming over him was a strange face. The lines blurred, then cleared slowly. The man over him was studying something, holding it up. Roger recognized it at last as a hypodermic syringe.

"Lenny?" he managed to say. Fear seized him. What was happening, what was the man doing?

"Right here," Lenny answered.

Roger managed to turn his head, bringing his eyes around to Lenny. "Who is he?" he asked weakly.

"He's a doctor. You've been sick," Lenny said, staring at him steadily, watching him.

Roger looked at the stranger again. It was not a pleasant face, but one that seemed cruel and hard, and in some way terribly frightening to him.

"Doctor Madison," Roger gasped. "Call Doctor Madison. The number—in my book. He'll take care...." The words were an effort.

"Sure, sure," Lenny said.

There was a faint prickling in his arm, and Roger vaguely remembered the hypodermic needle. He tried to struggle. He didn't want whatever it was they were giving him. He didn't want anything from this man. He had never seen a doctor like this one, so ruthless and unpleasant looking, wearing a dirty sweatshirt. That was no way for a doctor to look or dress.

He was slipping back again, however, falling away from them. He tried to reach out, to hold on to Lenny, but his hands were too heavy to move, and the blackness swept him away with it once more.

* * * * * * *

Silence. Not a sound to be heard in the room. Roger opened his eyes. He felt so dizzy, so light headed. He tried to lift his head, but it ignored the commands of his brain. He concentrated, straining, and at last his body began to respond—slowly, and painfully, but it did respond. He managed to lift his head from the pillow, squinting to see the room, to see if anyone was there.

No, he was alone. There was no one in the room with him—no Lenny, no awful doctor. Memory of the doctor came back to him then fully, in stark clarity. It was like a shock of cold water that helped to clear his mind.

Doctor Madison, he thought, pulling himself up on one elbow, I'll call Doctor Madison. He didn't want that other man caring for him. Lenny would understand now that he could talk again and explain. Lenny would like Doctor Madison, and Madison would take care of everything. He would know what to do about the dizziness and the pain, and this terrible falling and spinning.

His breath seemed to be exploding in his chest. It was a superhuman effort just to hold himself up like this on one elbow. How was he going to reach the phone?

He remained still for a moment, trying to get his breath back. The room had started to sway again. It steadied itself after a moment, but he felt as though his body were made of lead, much too heavy for him to move. Perhaps if he waited for Lenny to come back, Lenny would call Doctor Madison for him. He would fight against the drowsiness, make himself stay awake until he could talk to Lenny.

Suddenly he was afraid to wait. Some sense of danger within him told him to call the doctor himself, and not wait for Lenny.

He gripped the side of the bed tightly, straining to pull himself up. At last he was sitting. For an awful moment, the room plunged and rocked violently, and he leaned his weight against the headboard and prayed that he would outlast the storm. It abated finally, and he could breathe again, and move.

"Slowly," he told himself in a whisper. "Take it very slowly and very carefully. The phone is near the bed. I can reach it from the bed. All I have to do is hold to the headboard and lean toward the table."

He turned his head toward the table, to reassure himself that the distance was indeed small. His eyes blurred and then focused again. No, he had been right with his first glance. The phone was not there.

He managed to look at the floor, and then slowly his eyes traveled about the room. The phone was gone. It was impossible, and yet it was true. His telephone had disappeared from the room.

With a low groan, he collapsed under his own weight, sinking helplessly back down onto the bed.

CHAPTER ELEVEN

He felt better when he woke again—far from well, but at least better than before. He remained incredibly weak, and still dizzy, but slowly, ever so slowly, he was regaining control of his body and his mind. He felt as though he had been on the threshold of death, and now he had returned, if only part way, to the realm of the living.

He could sit now, although still with some effort, and the room remained fairly steady. His throat was still dry and parched, and his bedclothes were fairly dripping with sweat.

What has happened to me, he wondered? He had been tired before, and under a strain, but that hardly accounted for the agony he had been through. It was like nothing he had ever experienced before, and so sudden. It had come upon him out of nowhere.

He thought of Doctor Madison, and then he remembered the telephone. He turned, a bit too quickly, in that direction. Yes, the phone really was gone. That was preposterous. How could the phone have just disappeared? Someone had removed it apparently. Yes, he could see the place down at the floor where the phone had been connected. There was nothing there now but wires, covered with tape. The phone had been disconnected—but why?

He felt a moment of terrible dread as that question hovered in his mind, and close on its heels, other questions: the sickness, so sudden and violent that he had barely survived it—the missing phone—and that dreadful doctor who hadn't looked like a doctor at all. What did it all mean? Or did it mean anything at all? Was he letting his mind, still not fully clear, imagine preposterous things?

The sound of the door startled him and he looked up with wide eyes, to find that Lenny had come into the room.

"You're awake," Lenny said simply, staring closely at him as he crossed the room.

"Yes." Was it concern that caused Lenny to watch him so closely, with such a curious expression? And, if not that, what then?

"Feeling better?" The gentleness with which Lenny stroked his forehead seemed genuine enough, surely.

"A little. I've been quite ill, haven't it?"

"Yes, you had us scared. Here drink this." Lenny offered a glass full of a brownish looking liquid. It smelled, as he brought it close to Roger's face, bitter and unsavory.

"What is it?" Roger held back.

"Some medicine the doctor left for you. It'll make you feel better." He was insistent with the glass, lifting it firmly to Roger's lips. Roger took a tentative sip, and found that it tasted every bit as terrible as it smelled.

"Come on, all of it," Lenny said, "You want to get well, don't you?"

Roger relented, taking another mouthful, which he forced himself to swallow, then another, until the glass was at last mercifully empty. Satisfied, Lenny set the glass on the bedside table.

"That doctor, who was he?" Roger asked, allowing himself to be lowered to the pillow again.

"A friend of mine. He'll see that you get over this, don't worry."

"I didn't like him," Roger said. "I want my own doctor, Doctor Madison."

Lenny shook his head. "Can't do that," he said. "It's not smart to change horses in the middle of the stream. Better stick with Ben until you get better."

"But I didn't like him," Roger insisted. Lenny remained unmoved by his protests.

Roger remembered the telephone, then, and asked, "What happened to my phone?"

Lenny had turned away as though to go, but he turned back now abruptly, his eye once again fixed on Roger's face. "Why?" he asked.

"Why?" Roger repeated, bewildered. "I noticed it was gone. What happened to it?" He felt again that sense of dread. Something strange was happening, but he could not sort it out in his beleaguered mind.

"I removed it," Lenny said. "You were sick. I didn't want the ringing to disturb you. When you're better, I'll put it back."

"Couldn't you put it back now?" Roger asked timidly, not wanting to create a scene. He knew how difficult Lenny could be. "Suppose I got worse, or something happened…?"

"I'll be here," Lenny said, "If anything should happen." He left without waiting for Roger to argue the point. Plainly, the subject was closed.

If Lenny remained inflexible, however, he proved also to be a devoted nurse. Roger was almost never alone during his waking hours. Whenever he returned from his frequent sleep, Lenny was there, coaxing him to drink the vile medicine, attending to his needs, and watching him carefully for any progress or setbacks.

For the most part, Roger improved. He found himself sometimes perfectly lucid and, although a bit weak, feeling pretty close to normal. There were other times, however, when he seemed to fall suddenly back into the helplessness of fainting and pain and insensibility.

He questioned Lenny about the nature of his illness, but Lenny evaded his question. Nor did he know if Lenny was only sparing him the details, or simply did not know the answers himself.

The very lack of information made Roger's illness seem vastly more serious to him, and he almost looked forward to the return of Lenny's doctor friend, so that he could question him.

The doctor, however, did not again make an appearance, and when Roger asked about this odd fact, Lenny explained that he talked to the doctor regularly and that he was kept well informed of his patient's condition.

"If he's needed, he will be here," Lenny assured him.

There were other odd matters for Roger to puzzle over, besides his illness. For one thing, the atmosphere about the house had undergone a considerable change. As he slowly recovered, he began finally to realize how quiet the house had become. Marty and Zak were conspicuous in the lack of evidence of their presence. The partying and boisterousness that had typified their time in the house seemed to have ended, and the house was now shrouded in an almost ominous silence, as though it and its occupants were waiting.

At first, Roger was flattered by the realization, interpreting it as a matter of their concern for him, just as he was flattered by Lenny's attention, but as it continued, it seemed to him less and less real, not at all right. It began, even, to assume a sinister quality that he found disconcerting.

Could he have been so totally wrong in judging the three of them, he wondered? Before, he had been virtually a slave to their whims, an object of loathing, he was sure, in their eyes. Now, strangely, that had changed to concern for him, regard and consideration that was totally out of character for them, or so it seemed to him.

And there was Lenny, always Lenny, who instead of a selfish, irresponsible young cad, had become, seemingly over night, a paragon of kindness and efficiency. It had become apparent that not only Roger's health, but the management of the entire house, were now securely in Lenny's strong young hands.

The confirmation of this came on one occasion when Roger had awakened from a particularly bad bout of fever. Lenny was there, as he usually was. There was the medicine to be taken, and the customary inquiries after Roger's condition.

"Here, I'll help you sit up," Lenny said, helping Roger to a sitting position.

"What's the occasion" Roger asked with faint humor. He had lost his sense of time, but it had been a while since he had felt well enough to sit.

"You'll have to sign these," Lenny said.

Roger was surprised to see a sheet of checks. He stared at them, recognizing them as his own. They were all blank.

"For what?" he asked uneasily.

"For bills. They've been accumulating since you took sick. They'll have to be paid."

"But these are blank checks," Roger said. "I should know the amounts, and what they're going for."

"I'll take care of that." Lenny's voice was steely. Roger tried to stare him down, but he could not.

"I'd rather you made them out first," he insisted.

He expected difficulty, one of Lenny's displays of stubborn temper. To his surprise, Lenny relented. He shrugged and removed the checks. Later, he returned with them filled in. Roger tried to study them, but his dizziness had returned and he could make little sense of the writing. Nonetheless, he stared at them for a long time, pretending to examine them.

In the end, however, he signed the checks. Lenny was right, of course, that the accounts must be paid, the house must be managed, and he was probably fortunate to have Lenny on hand to look after everything so efficiently while he was unable to. Still, he could not help wondering which of them had won the round. Had he deceived Lenny into thinking he had really examined the checks?

Later, he decided that he had not. There were more checks, and this time he was much sicker, scarcely able to sit even with Lenny's help. He signed as instructed, wondering if his signature would even be legible. It was not until afterward, when his mind had cleared slightly, that he questioned whether this second group of checks had been filled in, or blank. He could not remember, and he hesitated to ask Lenny. To do so would be to admit to Lenny that he had no control over the money that Lenny was now spending for him.

How much money, he wondered anxiously, had been spent? Perhaps he should ask to examine the checkbook, when he was better—but when would that be? He seemed to have suffered a reversal, and now instead of improving, he was gradually weakening again. His moments of lucidity were fewer and less frequent, and he spent more and more of his time in a limbo world somewhere between sleep and consciousness. The medicine, which Lenny administered more and more often, seemed to be accomplishing nothing, and he said as much to his nurse.

"It's helping," Lenny assured him, and increased the quantity, to Roger's displeasure.

Roger's fears returned to him, gnawing at him during his waking hours. What kind of doctor was this friend, who never came to examine his patient? Why wouldn't Lenny call in Doctor Madison? For that matter, surely he was sick enough to be removed to a hospital. But even as fear stirred up these questions in his mind, it also made him hesitant to mention them to Lenny.

What was happening in the house outside his room? He had no idea what condition the house was in, and this fact caused him increasing concern. He even hinted that he was bored with the room, and asked that he be allowed to spend some time downstairs, but Lenny quickly dashed that hope.

"Too risky," he said firmly. "Ben says you're to stay in bed, period."

It seemed to Roger that he was signing an unusual number of checks. Surely there could not be this many bills. There never had been in the past, but when he tried to remember clearly how often the sheets of checks had been brought to him, or how many checks he had signed, he could not sort the information out in his mind. He even attempted to protest on one occasion, but Lenny insisted, even placing the pen in his hand and guiding the pen to the paper, so that Roger relented and signed once again, but he was becoming more and more frightened.

What if the money were all gone, what then? Was the money the real reason for Lenny's new consideration? He had been flattered by the change in attitude toward him. Now, with growing fear, he realized that he was more fully their prisoner than before. He was a slave to this bed, limited to this one room, while they were free to do whatever they wished with the house and its furnishings, with his money, even with his life. And this last thought was the most terrifying of all.

What was this strange sickness that had come upon him so suddenly, leaving him so totally helpless? For that matter, what was the medicine he now took in vast quantities, that seemed not to help at all.

His fear led him to a desperate thought. He woke on one occasion to find the room empty, and the glass of vile liquid on the table beside his bed. Apparently Lenny had brought it while he was asleep, and had left it there for later.

In a flash of intuition, Roger took the glass and, supporting himself weakly by the bedpost, he emptied the glass under the bed, where the bedclothes would conceal the stain. After that, he slept more easily. He heard Lenny come into the room after a bit, and he pretended that he was still asleep, watching through nearly closed eyes.

Lenny came to stand over him, studying him for a moment with a curious expression. He noticed the empty glass and picked it up. He looked curiously at Roger again, as though dubious. Then, apparently deciding that Roger must have taken the medicine on his own, he left, carrying the glass with him.

Roger was relieved that his ruse had been undetected, but he was more frightened now than he had been before—frightened, paradoxically, by the fact that his health improved. He had not taken the medicine, and as a result, he immediately felt much better.

CHAPTER TWELVE

There was something wrong with the medicine, He was convinced of that now. Far from improving his condition, as it was supposed to do, it was plainly making him ill.

He tried to avoid taking anymore of it, but whether he was suspicious or just being careful, Lenny did not again leave the medicine for Roger to take alone, but made a point of being there each time to watch him. Roger protested, suggesting that perhaps he should begin to cut down on it, but Lenny insisted. Roger had no choice but to take it, and each time, he now observed, it was followed by a worsening of his condition.

What was it, that vile brew that was being forced upon him? Drugs? Poison? And why? Did they mean merely to keep him their prisoner while they looted the house of its contents and drained his bank account? Or did they have some even more sinister scheme in mind?

His periods of consciousness had become agonies of terror. Where previously he had looked forward to seeing Lenny in the room, he now suffered almost unbearable fear each time he looked upon that handsome face, so cool, so impassive.

It was a conversation with Lenny that brought the fears very nearly to the stage of panic, and convinced him that he was the helpless victim of creatures more loathsome than ever he could have imagined.

It came up suddenly, out of the blue. Roger was seated in bed, eating the soup that Lenny had brought him. Lenny was standing idly by the window, fingering the brocade draperies absentmindedly.

"You have fire insurance, don't you?" Lenny asked without turning from the window.

Roger started so violently that he spilled the soup cross the coverlet. He dabbed at it with his napkin, his hands shaking fearfully.

"Why do you ask that?" he said, trying to sound casual and unperturbed.

"Just curious. This old house is a firetrap. I suppose your mother is the beneficiary."

"The estate. Everything goes to the estate," Roger said, and immediately regretted telling him that. It was as though he were walking a tightrope, every step carrying him into greater and greater danger. If only he were better, could think more clearly…if only he did not have to take that "medicine."

Afterward, the conversation fanned the flames of his terror. Why should Lenny think of fire, and ask about insurance? Was it only an idle curiosity, or was it a clue to what they were plotting? Destroy the house? Yes, if they had looted it, they could partially conceal their crimes by burning it down, although surely an investigation would eventually reveal the truth.

If that were their plan, though—a fire that would destroy the house—what did they have in mind for him? Was he somehow to be removed from the house first? Or did they plan to conceal what they had done with him as well. He was convinced by now that they had robbed and looted him as fully as the house. If they left, and left him behind, they risked his going to the authorities with the story of what they had done. Surely they must realize that no threat of scandal or reprisal could make him over-look the total theft of his money and belongings—unless they planned to leave no clues behind, living or otherwise.

Fear eventually gave him the courage that he needed to cope with the situation. His life was in danger, he was sure of it, and the instinct to live rose up in him. Somehow, he had to escape them, defeat their plans.

For once, Fate seemed to take his side. Having made his decision to take action, any sort of action, Roger was given the opportunity. Lenny brought in his medicine soon afterward and, before making Roger take it, went into the bathroom. Roger seized his chance without hesitation, and hurriedly emptied the glass under the bed. He lifted the empty glass to his lips just as Lenny reentered the room, and pretended to swallow before he set the glass on the table again.

"Take it already?" Lenny gave him a suspicious look. "I thought you hated taking that stuff?"

Roger managed what he hoped was a nonchalant shrug. "It does me no good to protest, does it?" he asked. "You always make me take it anyway. Might as well get it over with, as quickly as possible."

He saw the quick way Lenny's eyes darted about the room, and he knew that Lenny half suspected the truth. He feared that Lenny would think to look under the bed, but he did not, and when Roger pretended to be falling asleep, Lenny left.

He had succeeded thus far. Beyond this point, he had no plans, except that he must somehow escape. Without the medicine, he might be able to make it from the house. If he could only get to the neighbors—he would not have to call the police, he could simply ask them to take him to a hospital, or call in his own doctor. After that, he would be all right.

Before he could get out of the house, however, he had to get out of the bed. It was an ordeal, but his certainty that to fail might mean his life gave him the necessary determination. At last he was able to stand, if none too steadily, and after what seemed hours, he staggered to the door.

* * * * * * *

The hall was empty and in darkness. He crept along its length, supporting himself by leaning against the wall. He thought carefully, remembering the layout. For the most part, the hall was without obstruction. Halfway down, there was a credenza. He would have to be careful not to bump it or to knock the candelabra from it, lest he attract their attention.

He was near the credenza now, he was sure of it. He paused and felt before him with his hand. Not yet. He moved forward, pausing with each step to feel along the wall.

150

I should have reached it before this, he thought anxiously. Of course, his judgment was no doubt off. Still, he was nearly to the stairs. There, just a few feet ahead of him, would be the door to Lenny's room.

The credenza was gone. They had moved it for some reason, or maybe they had taken it from the house altogether.

He reached the stairs at last. Beneath him, light spilled from the parlor into the lower hall. Were they there? If so, how was he to get past that room without being seen? He made his way slowly downward, step by step, clinging to the banister for support. Below him, everything was still.

He had nearly reached the bottom when Lenny spoke from within the parlor, his voice sounding so loud to Roger's ears that he jumped and nearly lost his balance. Heart in throat, he pressed himself against the opposite wall, shrinking back into the shadows.

"I don't like the way it's going," Lenny said. "First Ben, now this shyster lawyer."

"Can't be helped." That was Marty. "We need the lawyer."

"And if it hadn't been for your carelessness, we would have had to call Ben in," Zak said sharply. "You nearly killed the old bird, and us with nothing set up yet. If it hadn't been for Ben, you'd have blown the whole thing."

"Okay, okay, so I'm not a doctor. I don't know about those things." Lenny was annoyed, that was apparent from the tone of his voice.

Roger felt his legs giving out. They were discussing him as though he were a cut of beef, or a piece of furniture. But what was it they were say-ing—the medicine—yes, he had been given too strong a dose, that had nearly killed him at the be-ginning, and Ben, who must really be some sort of doctor, had been called in to save his life. But, why? That made no sense. What were they planning? Who was the lawyer, and what did he have to do with all this?

He had broken out in a sweat. The strength that had enabled him to get this far was failing him fast. He had to do something, to go somewhere, but the open door of the parlor had him trapped.

"...Never get away with that. You aren't his nephew, and you would never convince his rela-tives." It was Zak, arguing some point that Roger had missed.

"I've already got that figured," Lenny replied. His voice seemed to Roger to be coming and going, losing and gaining volume so that it was becoming harder and harder to follow the conversation. "I'm his houseboy, remember? He's eccentric. The neighbors can testify to that, lots of other people, too, the pool workmen, the woman in charge of that Ball, everyone's seen how goofy he's gotten lately. It's not unusual for people like him to get very at-tached to servants. You read about it all the time."

"Maybe," Marty said, sounding doubtful. "Do you think he'll sign?"

The voices faded again. Roger felt himself swaying weakly. He clutched at the banister, trying desperately to support himself. He would have to go back upstairs, or find some place to hide until they had left the parlor.

"...In the fire...."

He caught the broken phrase, and his heart leaped into his throat. Fire, that subject again. It couldn't be coincidence. Somehow, that was part of their plan for him. He had to escape, had to hide himself until he could flee the house.

He turned toward the upstairs again. His legs seemed to be made of jelly. They refused to support him or to obey his wishes. His hand slipped on the railing. He reeled, trying to maintain his balance, but the stairs were rocking and swaying now. With a gasp, he felt consciousness slipping from him.

He fell, the blackness devouring him even before he struck the stairs.

* * * * * * *

Nameless phantoms pursued him through the nightmare world of blackness and pain. This time there was no relief in returning to consciousness. There were only scattered fragments of reality, moments when he seemed almost aware, but he could not bring his mind to function as it should.

"Drink this," Lenny's voice commanded him, and he drank. "Sign this," and he signed. What had it been, more checks? No, something larger, like a lease or a contract—it came to him finally as he felt consciousness returning at last…it had been a will. He had signed a will. He did not have to wonder what it said, or what it meant for him.

"You've been foolish," Lenny whispered in his ear. "You tried to get out of bed, but it's all right now. Lenny is here."

They didn't know, then, that he had heard them. But their ignorance offered him little hope. He was still totally within their power, and firmly convinced that they meant to see him dead. Perhaps this time he would not awaken, perhaps they had already accomplished their goal.

For all he knew, he might already be dead.

* * * * * *

The others were gone from the house, Marty and Zak. He was sure of it. A deathly silence had descended over the place, so complete that at first Roger found himself fancying that they had all gone, Lenny with them. There was nothing but the occasional weary creaking of the house itself, as though it too felt it could endure no more.

Maybe they've changed their minds, he thought in a burst of hope. Perhaps they had seen the dangers inherent in their schemes. They were the schemes of madmen, after all, schemes that could never have worked. Except that he would not have been around to see the failure.

He tried to imagine how the house looked. They would assuredly have stripped it of everything of value. He dreaded facing the result, and yet suddenly he felt it imperative that he should do so.

He tried to sit. The first attempt was a failure. He had been taking the medicine again, and he fell backward heavily against the bed, bumping his head painfully. He lay for a few minutes, re-gathering his strength, and tried again. This time he managed to sit up, if a bit unsteadily. He held himself there, preparing for the massive task of getting his feet to the floor.

It was while he was sitting, hands braced against the edge of the bed, that he heard the footsteps on the stairs. He was not alone, after all. Someone still remained in the house, was coming down the hall toward his bedroom, and there was little question in his mind as to the purpose of the visit.

He sank weakly to the bed again, just before the door opened, to reveal Lenny standing there. How beautiful he looked, Roger thought. How beautiful, and how deadly.

"You're awake?" Lenny greeted him.

"Yes. I just woke up," Roger said. Did Lenny know of his suspicions?

Lenny came nearer the bed and stood smiling down at him with an expression that appeared incredibly sweet and tender. Even knowing, as Roger did, what cruelty and ruthless cunning was concealed by that mask of innocence, he was nearly duped again into trusting.

"You were a naughty boy," Lenny said, "You got out of bed." He put a hand on Roger's forehead. "And you fell on the stairs. Had you been there long?"

"No," Roger lied. "I just wanted to surprise you. I thought I could make it, but I fell halfway down."

Roger's brain was awhirl. Lenny seemed to accept the statement, that was something, but what was their plan? He had heard only bits of conversation. If only he could remember it all, but his mind was still too clouded, his thoughts like slippery eels that evaded his grasp.

Fire—yes, they had mentioned fire, but surely that could not be their plan, not once they had discussed it fully. There was too much possibility that he might escape, or at least reach a telephone. And if they had cut all the phone wires, or any thing of that sort, why, that would automatically make the fire suspect. Even they must realize that.

"Marty and Zak?" he managed to ask.

"Are gone. They've gone ahead, to California," Lenny said. "It's time for your pill." His arm went under and about Roger's frail shoulders, helping him to the sitting position he had struggled so hard to achieve only a few minutes earlier.

"Here, take this," Lenny said, in the coaxing tone one would use to address a stubborn child. He held out a blue and white capsule.

"What is it?" Roger took it in a trembling hand. Poison, he thought—no, that was unlikely, that would be too easily discovered.

"Just something to make you sleep soundly," Lenny said.

Roger's hand jerked. He turned wide and imploring eyes toward Lenny's smiling face.

"But I sleep so much already," he pleaded. That was it, of course, a sleeping draught that would leave him in a deep stupor while the house burned down around him, so deeply asleep that he would die unaware of the blazing inferno.

"But you don't sleep well," Lenny said. "You toss and turn, and you have all those nasty dreams, remember? The doctor said this would let you sleep very soundly. You won't have to worry about those dreams any more." He smiled again, sweetly.

He urged Roger's hand insistently upward. Roger was frightened of taking the capsule, and even more frightened of not taking it, of what would happen. He knew how vicious this smiling young

156

man could be. Reluctantly, he placed the pill in his mouth. Lenny produced a glass of water, and Roger drank from it, swallowing hard, once, twice.

"There, that's better." Lenny relaxed visibly now that the medicine had been taken. He replaced the glass quietly on the nightstand, and patted Roger's hand comfortingly. "Now, I'll sit here with you until you fall asleep, so you won't get frightened."

Roger tried to look grateful, though he was worried about the capsule that was still in his mouth, lodged between gum and cheek. Soon enough the capsule itself would dissolve. If he were going to dispose of it without swallowing it, he would somehow have to escape those watching eyes.

The idea came to him at last, like a flash of light. It was a slim chance, and if it failed, he would no doubt suffer bitterly for it, but if it succeeded.... He tried to not to think of the consequences.

He met Lenny's steady gaze with a plaintive look. "I'm such a sentimental old fool," he said hoarsely, "But I was wondering if you would do something for me?"

"Maybe? That depends." Lenny was still suspicious, taking no chances.

"Mama's jewels. They were always so dear to me. I'd like to see them again, to hold them close to my heart, just for a moment...." He let his voice trail away and closed his eyes.

"You know I can't call you mother and ask her to come here. Why, think how upset she'd be if she saw you like this."

Roger's eyes flew open again. "Oh, no, she doesn't have them. Not all of them, that is. The best ones, the real family treasures, are still here. We hid them where we knew they'd be safe."

"You mean they're here, in this house?" There was no mistaking the sudden interest in Lenny's voice. He leaned closer, hanging on to every word. "But, I've been all through the house. Where are they?"

"They're…you promise you'll never tell anyone about this?"

Lenny nodded.

"They're in the attic," Roger said quietly.

Lenny's eyes automatically flew upward, to the ceiling of the room. "An attic? I didn't realize—but, how do you get to it?"

There's a back stair. There used to be a door on this floor, but that was sealed off long ago, and plastered over. And the one on the first floor is rather hidden, because we never use those stairs, you see. The broom closet, you know, the one in the utility room?"

"Yes," Lenny said eagerly.

"At the back of that—the back wall is a door. You'd never notice, unless you were actually looking for it. It's locked, but the key is on the hook inside the closet."

"And that takes me to the attic?" Lenny said, impatient to be on his way. "Where are the jewels?"

"Oh, you'll have no trouble finding them once you get to the attic. You'll see a large trunk. Mama left a lot of her more valuable things in it, but it's just the jewels that I want. The diamond tiara, especially. I do so want to see that again. It's from Tiffany's. They made it especially for her."

"Don't worry, I'll get them for you." Lenny gave him a confident smile and, without waiting for a reply, he turned and left the room quickly. His footsteps went at a rapid pace, almost running, down the hall.

Roger smiled grimly to himself. Yes, if there was one thing that you could depend upon, it was the greed of people like Lenny. It was their great and driving passion, their unchanging *raison d'être*.

Pulling himself up on one elbow, Roger spat violently, casting the partially dissolved capsule and its bitter contents across the bed. With a shaking hand, he took the water glass from the nightstand and washed his mouth out thoroughly, spitting the water onto the bed as well. It wouldn't matter if he ruined the bedspread. If his idea failed, nothing would ever matter for him again.

He thought of the back stairs, closed off for years because they were so dangerously flimsy, the wood all but rotted through. Would they be flimsy enough? Was Lenny's weight enough to make them crumble? It was a slim chance, but the only one he had.

He began to struggle from the bed. If he could manage to get downstairs, to the front door. Even if Lenny survived the stairs, the trip to the attic, there might still be a chance for him, if he could get outside, scream for help....

His heart rattled mercilessly in his chest, his breath had become a painful and Herculean labor. He was out of the bed at last, his feet on the floor, and by supporting his weight on the bedpost, he could stand.

The distance to the closed door seemed to stretch before him like a vast wasteland. He would have to cross that terrible space, travel the length of the hall, make the doubly dangerous journey down the stairs.

No, the thought came to him suddenly, if he could just find a phone—they had removed the one from his room, but there had been one as well in his mother's room, directly across the hall. Perhaps they had not thought of that. Perhaps they had not dreamed that he would ever make that journey.

Slowly, swaying with each movement, he began to inch toward the door. He held to the bedpost as long as possible—then, eyes wide with terror, he took a step forward without support. The room seemed to swim about him. He toppled forward and his clawing hands grasped at the post at the foot of the bed, and he managed to stay upright.

Another step, and then another. How far would Lenny have gone by now? Surely he must have reached the stairs, must have found the key. The house remained ominously silent.

I must hurry, Roger told himself, summoning all of his faint strength. He swayed, stumbled, caught himself, stumbled again, and this time, fell against the doorframe. He had made it across the room.

His hand was shaking so violently that he was scarcely able to open the door. It gave at last, swimming inward to reveal a short stretch of the hall. For an awful moment, Roger expected to see Lenny waiting for him, aware all the time of the ruse, but the hall was empty.

He heard the steps then, heavy and rapid, over-head. Lenny was in the attic. He had made the ascent up the stairs without mishap. He was in the attic now, looking for a trunk that wasn't there. There was nothing in the attic, hadn't been for years.

In another moment, Lenny would realize he had been tricked, and then he would come racing back, violently angry, no longer caring to play games.

Panic gave Roger new strength. He nearly ran across the hall, falling heavily against the door of the room that had been Mama's in the past. The knob turned, and he was inside, and there, across the room, was the telephone. If only there were time to phone the police, to explain. Even if Lenny succeeded in killing him, he would be trapped in his own evil.

Overhead, the footsteps had come to a halt. Abruptly, they started again, moving quickly back toward the stairs. Lenny was returning.

With a gasp, Roger staggered toward the phone. The receiver slipped from his fingers, fell to the floor. He fell with it, sinking to his knees, leaning his head against the bed. He dialed the operator, waiting in an agony of suspense for the cool, efficient voice to answer.

"The police," he croaked hoarsely when she finally answered. He waited, ears strained for telltale sounds, eyes glued to the doorway in which, any moment now, Lenny would appear.

At first, it seemed like an earth tremor, or the shaking produced by the jet airplanes when they took off from the nearby airport. The house shook slightly, as though waking from a deep slumber. Then came the crash, the awful rattling and banging of wood and metal and concrete, and with it, the spine-chilling scream that echoed through the hollow corridors of the house, long after it had ended so abruptly.

"Hello, hello, can I help you?" a voice was saying in his ear, "This is the police, can I help you?"

The police—Roger had nearly forgotten that he had called them. "Yes," he said into the phone, trying to make his voice sound more natural. "This is Mr. Caldwell. Roger Caldwell."

"Oh, yes, what can we do for you, Mr. Caldwell?"

Roger smiled at having his name recognized. Pleasant, that—it seemed to restore him to his rightful place. The place so long denied him.

"There's been an accident, I'm afraid," he said, "My, my houseboy, he's been in an accident. Dreadful thing. I fear he might be—he might be dead. It was quite a nasty fall."

ABOUT THE AUTHOR

Lecturer, former writing instructor and early rabble-rouser for gay rights and freedom of the press, **VICTOR J. BANIS** *is the critically acclaimed author ("...a master storyteller"—*Publishers Weekly*) of more than 140 published novels and nonfiction works, and his verse and short pieces have appeared in numerous journals (*Blithe House Quarterly, Fall 2006*) and anthologies (*Charmed Lives, Lethe Press, 2006*). Many of his books are being published by the Borgo Press Imprint of Wildside Press.*

www.ingramcontent.com/pod-product-compliance
Lightning Source LLC
Chambersburg PA
CBHW051921240626
47153CB00004B/1315